Love Bites

RACHEL K. BURKE

Harper
impulse

Harper*Impulse* an imprint of
HarperCollinsPublishers Ltd
1 London Bridge Street
London SE1 9GF

www.harpercollins.co.uk

A Paperback Original 2015

First published in Great Britain in ebook format by Harper*Impulse* 2014

A catalogue record for this book is
available from the British Library

ISBN: 9780008127428

Automatically produced by Atomik ePublisher from Easypress

Chapter 1

What do you do when you fall in love with your best friend's boyfriend?

There it was: the question I had been asking myself since that first day. The day I met him.

The day that changed everything.

It was the question I had analyzed endlessly, hoping to find some sort of answer. The only problem was, there was no answer. Because when you're forced to choose between the two people you love most in the world, either way you lose.

Sure, I know what you're thinking. Best friends don't fall in love with each other's boyfriends. They can't. It's an unspoken rule. Even if the guy is downright perfect, the fact that he's with your best friend prohibits you from falling for him.

Right?

I can honestly say that anyone who believes this has never, ever felt the way that I felt about David Whitman.

My name is Justine Sterling. I grew up in Rockland, Massachusetts, a small town south of Boston that most people have never heard of. With a population of under 20,000, there wasn't much to do in Rockland growing up, but when you're young, you have no idea how much of the world you're missing. I thought the rest of the world was just like Rockland. I imagined kids all over America living their lives exactly the way we did – riding bicycles, walking to the local convenience store, begging our parents to drive us two towns over to the nearest shopping mall.

For me, Rockland was the greatest place on Earth.

Still, there was always something missing, and I finally discovered what that was when I met Renee Evans. I never held an interest in sports or cheerleading, so in a limited-activity town like Rockland, my happiness stemmed from new CDs, new clothes, new posters. Only I never realized how much more fun those things were when you had someone to share them with. Someone who appreciated them just as much as you did.

I met Renee during my freshman year of high school. She had just transferred from a local Catholic school, and seeing as how Rockland High didn't have many new students, she was immediately scrutinized and labeled "the new girl." Everyone in Rockland had grown up with one another, and their families had grown up with one another. No one left Rockland. It was an intimidating place to start over.

When I first met Renee, she was a mess. Catholic school clearly didn't exemplify fashion. Her hair was blonde and thick, and ended abruptly at her shoulders. It looked similar to the way a horse's tail would look if you cut it to be six inches long. Like a bush that only grew sideways. And even worse, she had bangs too. I remember wondering what on earth had possessed her mother to give her that haircut, as her hair wouldn't have been that bad if it was long and weighed down. We didn't have hair-straighteners back then.

Looking back now, it makes sense to me. Mrs. Evans, Renee's mother, was a very sweet woman, but fashion was not one of her strong suits. As teens, Renee and I labeled her mother's sweater collection the "Bill Cosby Sweaters." Each of them shared the same blend of neon colors, knit together like an afghan. So it was of no surprise that Renee showed up to Rockland High her first day looking like she'd just stepped out of the Salvation Army.

2

Even worse than her hair were her clothes. They weren't bad per se, just much too big for her. It was like someone had dressed her up as a boy and forgot to tell her. Baggy clothes were the style in the nineties, with it being the grunge decade and all, but there were still ways to maintain your feminism.

What I liked about Renee was that she didn't seem to care. She was naturally pretty, but she didn't know it. She didn't give a second thought to her appearance. She was so happy to get the hell out of Catholic school and surround herself with normal people that she just took it all in. She was like a kid at Disneyland. She didn't say much. She didn't try to impress anyone. She just observed.

After striking up a conversation with her, I learned that this little fashion-deprived creature was actually quite intelligent. She knew a lot about music. More than anyone I'd ever met. I think she was so isolated at her previous school that she befriended rock and roll and never left its side.

I asked Renee once about Catholic school. She said that the kids were nice, just different. She told me that she wore an Aerosmith shirt to school on a casual day and all the kids teased her, chanting that Steven Tyler looked like an old lady. She said, "All I could think was that Steven Tyler was one of the most beautiful men I'd ever seen." It didn't bother her that the kids made fun of her. She just seemed genuinely confused as to how these people could view the world so much differently than she did. I think it was then that I fell in love with her.

Over time, Renee's image slowly began to develop. We went shopping at the local favorites, Hot Topic and Newbury Comics. We bought blue mascara and purple lipstick, oversized moonstone rings and bicycle-chain necklaces. We replaced Renee's skateboarder pants with tighter jeans, and her baggy band t-shirts with fitted ones. She grew out her bangs and put layers in her hair to offset the bush look.

And thus, Renee Evans was born.

Ironically, if you met Renee now, you'd never guess that she once dressed like a lumberjack. She has a very tall, modelesque presence, perfectly put together, like a stylist dressed her. Her thick hair is always immaculately curled, her makeup like a cosmetic ad, her scarves and boots matching the exact shades of her latest ensemble. But back then, Renee didn't care what people thought of her. She didn't try to fit in. Renee was who she was, without apology. And I loved her for that.

I fell in love with David Whitman the first time I saw him. It sounds ridiculous, I know, but trust me, no one thought the concept of love at first sight was more ridiculous than me. Up until David, I was a self-proclaimed serial dater. Renee was more of the relationship type, and she somehow managed to find great guys who also happened to be single. I never had such luck. I always found the ones who were single for a reason. Needy, jobless, womanizers, alcoholics, not-really-single-pretending-to-be-single, you name it. Deep down, I wanted to find true love, but it just never worked out that way.

Renee always teased me for my ever-changing love life, calling me a game player, telling me I loved the thrill of the chase. But the truth was, I hated dating. I hated the disappointments. That's what dating was: one disappointment after the other. I guess I just hoped that eventually I'd find someone who would make all the bad dates worth it.

And I did. I just didn't expect him to stroll through my living-room door with my best friend.

David Whitman. Renee had told me all about him. In fact, he had been the sole point of our conversations for weeks. When Renee had a new love interest, it was all she talked about. At the time, we were both seniors at UCLA, and Renee was interning at *Pace*, a local LA magazine. David was the sports editor, and every day Renee came home with a new story about him – what he was wearing that day, how he'd brought her a coffee, how all the girls in the office loved him. That was the funny thing about Renee.

4

She called me a game player, yet she generally only liked a guy if a) he didn't like her, or b) everyone else liked him. So essentially, she played games too, she just didn't know it.

Before I met David, I wasn't sold on the idea of him. Renee was a creative soul. A creative soul who was now dating a sports editor. She hadn't mentioned a single thing they had in common, or that she found interesting about him. It seemed to me that she felt she had won the hunk of the office and wanted to parade around with the prize on her arm. Sure, he sounded nice and cute and all, but I knew Renee. Eventually, she'd want more than that.

When David walked through my living-room door that first night, everything in my body stood still. I understood now. None of his personal history or interests mattered. It was the effect he had on you. Those eyes. That smile. He could be a needy, jobless, alcoholic womanizer and it wouldn't have mattered. You would have followed him to the end of the Earth anyway.

From the instant I met David, I felt an immediate connection that I had never experienced before. It was the way he looked at me. Maybe he looked at everyone that way, but he still made me feel like I was the only person in the room. Intense brown eyes and the faintest hint of a smile on his lips. Like he was looking through me. Like he knew that he could have me if he wanted me, even if it meant ruining a lifelong friendship. He had that power.

I hated him for that.

And at that moment, for the first time in my life, I hated my best friend.

Chapter 2

Los Angeles, CA
January 2009

During our senior year at UCLA, shortly after Renee landed an internship at Pace, I landed one of my own at Sphinx, a local video-game company. I have no idea why they hired me, because I didn't love video games. I didn't even like video games. I was just desperate for a paying internship. But as it turned out, Sphinx was exactly what I was looking for.

After several major switches, I'd decided on communications because it allowed me to take photography courses, which had always been my true passion. I loved photography because it was the only art that allowed you to capture truth in the visual sense. Renee loved music because it captured truth in the audio sense, but for me, I loved the visual. The lens didn't lie. It highlighted the little beauties of everyday life that were often overlooked, and there was something so raw and honest about that. But I also knew that photography was a difficult business to earn a living at, therefore I picked a major that included creative courses that still had a business aspect to them, such as marketing and media studies.

I had just completed an interactive marketing course on social media outreach, as well as a media literacy course in which we were assigned to read about the psychology behind role-playing video games. So when I came across Sphinx's ad stating they were looking for interns with experience in online marketing and knowledge of video games, it sounded pretty perfect. I may not have been much of a gamer, but my last two classes had provided me with all the knowledge I needed for the position. Not to mention, it paid a lot. More than most internships.

Before I was called in for an interview with Sphinx, I was contacted by a local health insurance company, HCG, who was looking for an intern to manage their website and social media pages. I like to call these kinds of experiences "blessings in disguise." Because if I hadn't had the opportunity for comparison, I never would've realized how utterly perfect Sphinx was for me.

The HCG office was located next to the LAX airport. I was greeted by a man named Jason Porter, who introduced himself as the Human Resources Director. He cleverly referred to himself as the resident "herd," then had to draw me a verbal map to his joke, spelling out the acronym for Human Resources Director: HRD. He chuckled at his own irony. I did not find him funny.

Jason brought me to his spacious office, then sat down at his desk and motioned for me to take a seat across from him. He began the interview with some small-talk, asking me why I moved to LA, why I chose my major, what courses I had taken thus far. As I answered his questions, I noticed that he was actually quite good-looking. Olive skin, green eyes, nice smile. I suspected he was older than he looked, as he had the slightest hint of gray in his brown sideburns. Early forties, maybe.

These good looks slowly disappeared less than ten minutes into the interview. After the small-talk concluded, Herd wasted no time getting down to business. He made it very clear that, when I was not in class, every spare moment would be spent working for him. On the days I did not have class, I would be expected to work a full eight-hour day, beginning at 8am, and wear a suit. I almost choked on my own disgust. I was not a morning person, nor was I a suit.

And five days a week? I had envisioned working a few afternoon hours after class, three days a week at most. Herd had other plans for me.

It only got worse from there. Herd went on to tell me that he expected the internship to become a full-time position once school was complete. He emphasized that he worked between fifty to sixty hours a week and expected this person to follow suit. No pun intended. He droned on about his role in the company and how much impact he'd had since he came on board. It wasn't even an interview. It was Herd talking for the sake of hearing himself talk. I couldn't get out of there fast enough.

When the interview was finally over, Herd handed me his business card and frowned when I placed it in my purse.

"You know, you should really buy a briefcase," he scoffed in a patronizing tone. "Placing business cards in a purse is just so... unprofessional." He laughed mockingly and shook his head, having his own little private business joke with himself. "And also, Justine, you should always wear a suit to an interview." He looked me up and down like I was a toddler who'd dressed herself for the first time. I followed his gaze, glancing down at my black-collared shirt and charcoal dress pants. Judging by his expression, you would've thought I'd shown up dressed for a hip-hop video.

As I headed toward the elevator, I passed by the work area, where all the insurance agents sat next to each other in tiny cubicles, wearing blazers and headsets. Their desks were lined with tiny bags of junk food. Most of them were overweight. They looked tired. I felt sad for them.

Herd shook my hand goodbye at the elevator, but I no longer saw him as good-looking. I saw him as a man with a condescending, insincere laugh, who had bags under his eyes from working sixty hours a week. A man with no social life and no family, only a mahogany desk and an oversized briefcase. A man who owned an expensive house with expensive things that never got used.

It's funny how, in the course of thirty minutes, you can learn very, very quickly what you want in life. And, more importantly, what you don't want.

As a precaution, I went out and bought a suit. I refused to be humiliated twice. Luckily, I didn't need it, as Sphinx was as far from a suit shop as you could get.

Sphinx's office was located in Playa Del Rey, which was about a 20-minute drive from my apartment in West LA. Their lobby was like a Toys-R-Us. The walls were covered with action figures and game posters. A giant candy bowl sat on the receptionist's desk. As I filled out my application, I continued to sneak glances at a Reese's peanut-butter cup that was taunting me from the corner of the dish. The receptionist finally noticed and offered me the dish. I liked the place already.

I watched the employees flow in and out of the lobby as I waited for my interview. None of them were dressed professionally. In fact, it was the complete opposite. Some of them had facial piercings and tattoos. They reminded me of the people who worked at Hot Topic when Renee and I shopped there in high school. A petite Asian girl wearing tights, jean shorts and boots skipped through the lobby, stealing a Kit-Kat from the candy bowl. I smiled at her.

After giving my application to the receptionist, a man appeared and led me to the interview room. He introduced himself as Manuel Mendoza, the Human Resources Manager. He was short and stocky, with a young face. Latino, I assumed by his name and dark features. He wore a gray t-shirt, jeans, and converse sneakers. He did not refer to himself as an acronym.

My interview was the complete opposite of HCG's. It didn't feel like an interview at all. Manuel and I briefly discussed the position and my college courses, then he brought me to the "gaming room," which held several flat-screen TV's hooked up to gaming consoles and a few old-school arcade games. I confessed that I didn't play video games. He didn't care. We played anyway. It was the best interview of my life.

After Manuel beat me at a round of virtual sword-fighting, he brought me back to the interview room and introduced me to Vincent

Seminari, Sphinx's Marketing Director. Manuel had warned me that Vincent was the man to impress, as he would be my future boss. Vincent had dark eyes, a long nose that gave him character, and spoke with a hint of an Italian accent. I guessed that he was probably in his early to mid-forties. He also wore jeans and informed me that everyone at Sphinx did. He joked that I was the "best-dressed person there." I felt foolish in my stupid suit. He told me that most of the employees began work at 10am and everyone received four weeks of paid vacation annually.

I was in my glory.

After the interview, Vincent gave me a tour of the building. The workstations were gorgeous. Sphinx occupied the seventh floor of the building, a bright, beautiful space with an incredible view of the city. There were no cubicles, only wide tables in the shape of a U, where everyone sat next to each other. Open and free. It was what every company should be.

As Vincent and I walked around, I noticed that everyone seemed happy. Two of the employees shot Nerf guns at each other from across the room. The break room had free coffee, snacks, and soda. The CEO walked through, clutching a skateboard in his right hand. It was like being in a world where no one grew up.

Before we reached the elevator, I noticed a small office that had paper taped over the window. I turned to Vincent, pointing to the room. Before I could say anything, he shook his head, laughing.

"You don't want to go in there," he insisted.

"Why not?" I asked.

"We call that the 'Lactation Station.'"

"The what?"

"Lactation Station," he repeated, lowering his voice to a whisper. "It's the breastfeeding room."

I had never laughed so hard in my life.

Chapter 3

I make lists. Correction, I'm a compulsive list-maker. I write everything down – to-do lists, shopping lists, future goals. And sometimes, when I'm down, I make them for simple inspirational reminders.

I stared at the piece of my paper in my hand for a long time; the new list that I would hang on my fridge and read every day as a positive reminder.

Why I Moved Back to Boston:

That was as far as I'd got.

Okay, so I wasn't adjusting well. It was November. I was freezing. My parents had a cottage in Cape Cod that they rented out during the summer, so they were letting me live there rent-free until summer rolled around again. Cape Cod was great in the summer, but in the winter it was the boonies. I had to drive 45 minutes to reach civilization, and even then, the only nightlife that existed on the south shore was at Irish pubs. I hated beer. I hated sports. I rarely ate meat. That didn't leave me many options. If I tried to order a hummus wrap and a Champagne Royale at one of the local bars, they'd think I was insane.

My cell phone rang before I could attempt to continue the list. I looked down at the ID and felt a slight pang of disappointment. I had been home for almost four months, and every time my phone rang, I still hoped it was him.

It never was.

"Hey girl," I answered.

"Hey J," Renee said on the other end. "You still coming to Dylan's show tonight?"

Shit. I had forgotten all about it. Renee's fiancé, Dylan, was the singer in a local band, and she had told me about the show weeks ago. I glanced down at my pajama pants. "Yeah," I answered. "Of course."

"You forgot, didn't you?"

"Yup." Renee always knew when I was lying. There was no point in covering it up. "What time does it start?"

"They go on at ten. They're playing the downstairs room at the Middle East, not upstairs. I'm going to ride in with Dylan so just call me when you get there and I'll come meet you."

"Okay. See you soon." I hung up and took a sip of coffee from the mug I'd been holding for the last 20 minutes. I picked up the piece of paper again.

Why I Moved Back to Boston:
#1 – Renee is here. She is my other half. I need her in my life.

It was true. LA didn't feel like home without Renee. Sure, I had made a few friends at school and at Sphinx, but for the most part, Renee and I did everything together. When she left, it didn't feel the same. And besides that, the girl was an absolute saint. How she could forgive me after what happened with David was beyond me. But regardless, she was my best friend, and she was here. Therefore I would brave the coldest of winters to be with her, because I loved her.

Truthfully, though, everything worked out for the best. Renee was now six months pregnant, engaged, and happier than I'd ever seen her. Dylan and Renee were perfect for each other. David and Renee… weren't. My aching heart wanted to say that he was perfect for me, but my head knew that wasn't true either.

#2 – David does not live here. Therefore, I do not have to worry about seeing him everywhere I go.

I swear, people in love need a live-in therapist. It's all we think about. It's all we talk about. After David broke up with me, I couldn't go anywhere. Everything reminded me of him. Our favorite restaurant, our local bar, the supermarket where we shopped. I couldn't go any of those places. It was almost as if it would've been better if he'd died in some tragic accident or something. At least then I wouldn't have to worry about bumping into him in line at Von's.

Here, I was safe. Nothing reminded me of him. He was thousands of miles away. It's like it was all a dream.

But deep down, I knew that as far away as I was from him, he was still here. He was always here. I couldn't escape him.

I glanced down at the paper again. I couldn't think of a number three.

Los Angeles, CA
February 2009

I always know that I'm going to sleep with a guy by the way he looks at me. It's usually an intense stare, he's usually Italian, and I usually end up regretting it. That's just how it goes.

I was less than an hour into our morning meeting at Sphinx when I noticed it. The Stare. I was seated in the conference room with the marketing team for their weekly conference. They met every Monday at 10am to go over marketing strategies for new game releases, and Vincent thought it would be a good idea for me to join the meetings,

13

even though I hadn't a clue about anything they were discussing. As one of the girls talked about an upcoming convention, I caught eyes with Vincent from across the table. I quickly reverted my gaze back to the girl so he'd think I was paying attention. I wanted to make a good impression. But when I looked back at him a few minutes later, he was still staring at me.

Oh boy.

It's easy to differentiate a professional stare from a sex stare. A professional stare ensures that the employee is comfortable and attentive on his or her first day of work, but seizes once eye contact is met. A sex stare does not. A sex stare is confident and will maintain eye contact even after the contact is broken, thus intimidating its target and causing he or she to become nervous.

And damn it, it always fucking works.

By the third eye-contact connection, I already knew I was going to sleep with him. The stare wasn't making me uncomfortable. Instead, a familiar nervous-yet-exciting stomachache appeared. I looked down at my outfit, trying to see myself as he did. I was wearing a black fitted sweater, my favorite pair of Bebe jeans, and black stilettos. Undoubtedly the most feminine outfit in our entire mini-gaming world. I twirled my long brown locks between my fingers. I felt his dark, Italian eyes on me. I liked it.

My eyes drifted to his left hand. No wedding band. Check. Rolex watch. Silver cufflinks. Double check. Navy collared shirt, tanned skin, slightly gelled hair. Very put-together. I pictured him in an expensive sports car. A Porsche, maybe. Black. I pictured myself in the passenger seat. I wondered if he had a girlfriend.

It suddenly occurred to me that maybe I had been looking in the wrong places. I mean, didn't a lot of couples meet at work? It was pretty obvious by now that I wasn't going to find Mr. Maturity at UCLA, nor was I going to find Mr. Monogamous on the Sunset Strip. Vincent was older, good-looking, and, judging from his appearance and title, did well for himself financially. He was a catch. And based on my appearance, age, and the burning stare from across the

14

conference table, it appeared that the feeling was mutual.

My first few weeks at Sphinx were a joke. I made zero professional contribution whatsoever. Instead, my days went something like this:

10am: Get coffee and bagels for Vincent.

11am: Have coffee and bagels with Vincent in his office. Pretend to talk about work. Talk about anything but work.

12pm: Have lunch with Vincent.

1pm: Pretend I am checking my professional emails. I am an intern. I do not have professional emails.

2pm: Pretend to pay attention to Vincent's social media tutorial when what I am really paying attention to is how close he is standing to me.

3pm: Attend "off-site meeting" (happy-hour drinks) with Vincent and "vendors." Pretend to know what "vendors" are.

Repeat.

Surprisingly, Vincent waited an entire month before asking me out. By then, I was practically panting for it. He, of course, pretended the invitation was to "celebrate" all the hard work I had accomplished during my first month. I knew better. Not only because he stared at me like I was a Krispy Kreme, but because I hadn't accomplished jack shit in the past four weeks.

The bad news was that he was going to be working from Sphinx's London office for the next month, so our date was postponed until his return. The good news was that we had already covered everything that you cover on a first date, so I figured I was good to skip the three-date rule and prematurely put out. I knew everything about him that I needed to know. He had grown up in Milano and moved to the United States when he was eleven. He lived in Beverly Hills. He had a ten-year-old son, whom he mentioned having on the weekends, thus the reason he didn't go out much. Ah, a divorced dad. I wondered if my parents would disapprove.

I couldn't wait to tell Renee about my upcoming date. I had been gushing about Vincent since my first day at Sphinx, and I could tell she was relieved that I finally had a love interest, too. Her daily David

Whitman anecdotes had grown more than tiresome and I hadn't even met the guy yet. They were still in the newlywed stage, where they mainly just had sex at his place. David lived alone. I understood.

I was bent over the kitchen stove making a grilled cheese when I heard the sound of our front door open.

"He asked me out!" I yelled to Renee, flipping my sandwich onto a plate. I barreled into the living room, but stopped dead in my tracks when I realized she wasn't alone.

"J," Renee said cautiously, as if she felt bad catching me off guard. "This," she gestured behind her, "is David."

Wow. I was not expecting that. Naturally, I wasn't expecting David to be standing in my living room, but I also wasn't expecting to feel the sinking in the pit of my stomach when I met him. Never in my life had I met someone and felt so instantly drawn to them. And he hadn't even said anything yet. He just grinned at me like we were having a private joke. The only two people in the room. In the universe.

"He asked you out, huh?" David joked. There it was again, that mischievous, one-dimpled grin. His eyes went slightly wild when he smiled, like he was scared, surprised, and amused all at the same time. I couldn't help but smile back.

"He did," I said, nodding slowly. David loomed behind Renee, at least six feet tall, with dark hair and a hint of a baby face. His lips had twisted into a faint smirk, the amusement of the situation still lingering. But those eyes. Those giant, brown, crazy eyes. They were having sex with me. In my own living room. Behind my best friend, who I could no longer see.

"About time," Renee said, hanging her purse on the wall rack. "Listen, we're going to sleep here tonight because David has a meeting in Brentwood in the morning. Fill me in tomorrow?" She winced like she felt bad.

"Okay," I agreed. David followed Renee out of the living room, still smiling back at me. But not with his mouth. With those goddamn eyes. I had never met anyone who could smile without moving their *mouth.*

I heard the bathroom door close and the sound of the sink running. Before getting settled on the sofa, I realized that I'd left my grilled cheese sandwich in the kitchen. I got up and headed toward the kitchen, and there he was. Leaning casually in the doorway, his right arm propped against the wood. Like he'd been hiding there, waiting for me the whole time.

"So, did you say yes?" he asked, not bothering to move out of my way. He was blocking the doorway. I couldn't get through. I didn't care. "To the date, I mean."

"I did." I was whispering. I wasn't sure why. Like we were sharing a secret.

"Lucky guy," he said in a low voice, slowly looking me up and down. As he turned and disappeared into Renee's bedroom, his eyes never left mine.

Even if Vincent wasn't in London, at that moment, he still seemed a million miles away.

Chapter 4

The Middle East felt like my childhood. It was what I imagined Seattle to be like during the nineties. Dark basement feel, sticky floors, heavy distortion, the distinct aroma of weed and beer. It was dirty and raw. In LA, everything was pretty. Even the rock clubs were pretty. In Boston, the rock scene was real, not manmade. No one painted a mural of Jim Morrison on the side of the building to be cool. It was cool without trying.

I spotted Renee as soon as I walked downstairs. Even at six months' pregnant, she was still stunning. Her blonde hair spiraled down to her waist, and she wore a long, black vintage coat with a fur collar. She looked like a seventies groupie. She was perched by the merchandise table, helping the merch girl unload the band's albums and t-shirts. Her face lit up when she saw me.

"Hey!" She waved and abandoned the table, wrapping me in a hug. "I'm so glad you're here. You *have* to see the albums!"

Tonight was the album-release party for Dylan's band, Electric Wreck. They had just finished their first full-length album, *Hiatus*. I'd photographed them for the album cover, thanks to Renee's referral, but had yet to see the finished product. Renee was like an elated toddler, grabbing me excitedly by the arm and dragging me to the table.

"What do you think?" she asked, thrusting a copy into my

hands. I looked closely at the cover. It looked great. We had used their studio for the shoot, which everyone agreed was a practical location, with the graffiti and equipment in the background adding to the sincerity of the setting. The four guys were strewn across the room with their instruments – Christian in the back of the photo behind the drum kit, Andy seated on the floor with a guitar in his lap, Jeff leaned up against the wall clutching his bass, Dylan in center, head down, gripping the microphone with both hands. It was a fantastic shot.

"It looks awesome," I said, running my fingers along the edges. I had sent the final image to their graphic designer, who had adjusted it to black and white and added classic-style font so it looked like an album from the sixties. I flipped it over to read the twelve-song list on the back.

"I know!" Renee was beaming. "I told him it would come out great."

Dylan was not a fan of the cover concept. He thought a photo of the band members was cheesy and opted for artwork instead. Renee insisted that, since they were all good-looking guys, it would be more marketable. Sex sells. Dylan argued that this theory was exactly what was wrong with the music industry today.

He eventually gave in.

With her new mom-to-be schedule, Renee had quickly become the band's pseudo-manager. She devoted all her spare time to learning about the music industry and indie artist success strategies. Thus, Dylan usually listened to her even when he didn't want to. And I was just grateful for the referrals. Electric Wreck was the second band she had referred to me for photography shoots, and since I hadn't found a job or a permanent place of abode yet, freelance work helped. Living rent-free also helped.

Although I knew the real reason for my lack of drive. I hadn't fully committed to being home yet. My heart was still in LA.

Renee handed a cardboard box to the merch girl, then led me to the side of the stage. "Did I tell you that they raised over

19

20,000 dollars for their album through the Kickstarter campaign?"

She had. At least three times. "I think so," I lied.

"You're almost as bad of a liar as I am," she said, laughing. "Sorry if I keep repeating myself, it's just so exciting. *Twenty thousand dollars!* They haven't even been around that long."

Through Renee's research, she'd discovered that a lot of emerging indie bands were launching online donation campaigns to help with their album recording expenses. Renee had started a campaign for the band and executed different marketing strategies to get the word out. I knew she'd put a lot of effort into it, but I don't think anyone realized how effective it was until the results came in. It was all Renee had talked about for weeks.

"Oh, I forgot to tell you," she said, lowering her voice. "Andy thinks you're cute. He hasn't shut up about you since the photo shoot. Do you…" She hesitated. "What do you think of him?"

I think he's not David, I thought.

"I hadn't really thought about it," I said. Technically, it was the truth. I hadn't thought about any man except David in months.

"Do you think he's cute?" she asked. She had a painful expression on her face, like it would hurt her if I said no.

I considered. Their guitarist, Andy, was average-looking, shaggy dirty-blonde hair, nice cheekbones, a little extra weight around his midsection. He was the personality of the band, that was for sure. Dylan was too intense, and the other two didn't talk much.

"He's okay," I answered, shrugging. "He's funny."

The truth was, every time I pictured myself with a guy, all I could think of was David. I couldn't imagine feeling that way with anyone else. And if I couldn't feel that again with someone, then everything else would just be settling. I'd rather be alone.

Just then, the lights dimmed and the four guys slowly made their way to the stage, Dylan arriving last. Renee's eyes locked on him, and I knew better than to say anymore. I had seen Dylan perform, and the way he silenced the audience. He had an undeniable gift. He wasn't just a voice, he was a presence. It was easy to see why

Renee had fallen for him.

When I first met Dylan, he wasn't at all what I had expected. Maybe because he was so different from David. He was smaller than I'd imagined, five foot nine at most, and incredibly skinny. A true starving artist. He had a big nose and very dark hair, almost black, the complete opposite of his glowing light-blue eyes. His eyes were so intense it was hard to look at him sometimes. Like he was perpetually scared.

After my first conversation with Dylan, I understood the attraction. It was his voice. Not his singing voice, but the way he spoke. He had a deep, sexy tone and spoke slowly and deliberately, like he was half-asleep. It was almost hypnotic. He kept you hanging on every word. Renee also had a tendency to gravitate towards the mysterious, detached type, and Dylan was about as elusive as they came. You never knew if he cared, what he was thinking. He just stared at you with those glowing eyes.

The music started, and for the next two hours, I had officially lost Renee. The music had taken her. My beautiful best friend, with her tiny baby belly poking out from behind her coat. Swaying to the music. In love.

Throughout the entire show, her eyes never deviated from Dylan. At one point, he looked over at her and smiled ever so slightly, and I felt a pang of jealousy in my gut. I wanted that. I wanted someone to look at me like that.

Only that someone was 3,000 miles away, and he'd never look at me like that. Because he didn't love me.

Los Angeles, CA
March 2009

David started coming around the house more often. I'd be lying if I said I wasn't thrilled. I tried not to be. I tried to pretend I wasn't excited by the sight of him on my couch when I came home, the thought of him in my shower. I tried not to read into his mild flirtations, not to feel his eyes on me constantly. I tried to fight it. I did.

I started to think that maybe it was in my head. Maybe I was reading into it. But it seemed like every time Renee stepped out of the room, he'd inch just a tiny bit closer to me, stare a little bit more intensely. And he didn't look away. The Stare.

One night, the three of us were watching a movie in the living room. Renee decided to go to bed early, and David stayed up to finish the movie with me. But he didn't watch the movie. He watched me. I felt his eyes on me the entire time, waiting for me to look his way. I didn't.

"Anyone ever tell you that you look like Denise Richards?" he finally asked.

"Every day of my life." My eyes were still on the TV.

He kept staring. I finally gave in and looked at him. He was grinning. That wild-eyed grin. That we're-sharing-a-secret grin.

"What?" I asked, fighting back a laugh. I couldn't help it. He had this way of staring and smiling like he knew something you didn't.

"You're really into this movie, huh?" he asked.

I stopped watching it a long time ago, I thought to myself.

"It's okay," I said.

"Have you ever had Rocky Road popcorn?"

I whipped my head in his direction. "Huh?"

He stood up, walked over to my chair and grabbed both of my hands with his. In one swift motion, he lifted me to my feet. "Come on," he said, pulling me behind him.

And there, in the kitchen, we melted chocolate and marshmallows, crushed almonds, popped popcorn, and threw them all together. David stood tall above me, so close we were almost touching, and without missing a beat, he shoved a giant fist of popcorn into my mouth.

I screamed, wiping chocolate and marshmallow wads from my face. We were both in hysterics. If this were a date, it would've been the best date I'd ever had.

The next day, Renee told me she wanted to break up with him.

Apparently, their differences were beginning to weigh on her, which I knew would happen eventually. You can't fight the inevitable. Up until David, Renee hated jocks. She wouldn't even look at a guy if he didn't hold an interest in some sort of creative endeavor. I think David's charm had succeeded in blindsiding her temporarily, but now graduation was creeping around the corner. She was starting to think about the future. And questioning whether or not David would be a part of that.

I couldn't fathom it. She had Him. How could you give up those eyes? Those dimples? The way you felt inside when he looked at you?

Then I realized why. She didn't feel that way. Maybe to a degree, but not nearly as close to the way I felt. I wouldn't have given him up for anything.

I understood where she was coming from, but deep down, part of me hated her. I had been on an endless bout of bad dates for as far back as I could remember, hoping to find what she already had. And she was going to throw it away, just because the guy didn't "get" rock and roll.

Since Renee relied heavily on my opinion, I did what any best friend would do. I told her the truth – that I thought David was great, but if she was having doubts, then maybe she should take some time apart from him to think about their relationship. Renee was flying home to Boston the following week to attend her grandfather's funeral, so she'd have some space to evaluate their future while she was away.

I just honestly didn't think that, in the end, she'd decide to stay with him.

Chapter 5

It was almost one in the morning by the time the band was packed up and ready to go. Everyone except for the venue employees and band members had already gone home, so I was left in the smoke-filled backstage room with the Electric Wreck guys while Renee was off settling their bar tab. Dylan must have sensed that I was uncomfortable, sitting alone in the corner, because just as I was about to leave he sat down next to me.

"You like the show tonight?" he asked.

"You know you're always great," I said, although I wondered if he really did. No matter how many compliments Dylan received, he still seemed to doubt himself. Typical self-loathing artist.

"Do you have to drive back to the Cape tonight?"

"Yeah. It's only a little over an hour. Not so bad."

"Except at this hour." He smirked. "You're always welcome to crash with us, you know."

Renee and Dylan lived in Quincy, which was only a 15-minute drive from the city, but I hated sleeping anywhere except in my own bed.

"I'll be okay," I said. "Thanks, though."

"How are you kids doing over here?" Andy asked, sliding in between Dylan and me. He removed a joint from his pocket and held it in my direction. "You smoke?"

I thought about it for a minute. I wasn't much of a pot-smoker because it made me sleepy, but I did have a long drive home...

"What the hell," I agreed. "Here?"

"My car. I think they're going to kick us out soon."

I followed Andy through the empty main room, catching Renee's eye on the way. She abruptly stopped her conversation with the bartender when she saw us leaving, giving me the thumbs-up sign. I made a joint-smoking motion with my hands so she wouldn't get the wrong impression. She shrugged and gave me a smile that said, *"Hey, it's a start."*

Andy drove a black Infinity with gray-leather interior. It was much nicer than I'd imagined. I guess I assumed all musicians drove beat-up vans like Dylan did.

"This is nice," I said, running my hand along the seat. It had that new-leather smell that I loved.

"Well, playing in a band isn't the only thing I do." He lit the end of the joint. "I also teach guitar lessons. And I taught music theory classes for years at the Art Institute."

I took the joint from his grasp, looking around before taking a hit. We were parked in the lot behind the club, a dark, inconspicuous place. I felt safe. "Why'd you quit?" I asked.

"If we're going to be touring more, I need the schedule flexibility. I'll go back to teaching once we start working on our next album, when I know I'll be home for a while."

I exhaled a ring of smoke into the air, feeling much more relaxed. That was the good thing about pot. It made your problems not seem so bad. David felt a million miles away.

"What are you smiling about?" Andy asked, looking at me with hazy eyes. I hadn't even realized I was.

I took another hit of the joint and shrugged. I was having too much fun in my little stoned world to start unleashing my weird thoughts. My head began to feel lighter. I wondered how long we'd been in the car. It felt like forever.

"Just smiling at life, huh?" Andy asked, stubbing out the joint

25

in his ashtray. It was the furthest thing from the truth, but at that moment, it felt one tiny step closer.

"Yeah," I said. "Something like that."

Los Angeles, CA
April 2009

The day had finally arrived. My long-anticipated date with Vincent was here at last.

And I had absolutely no idea what to wear.

He hadn't mentioned where he was taking me, but I assumed it was somewhere fancy, so I had to dress to impress. The problem was, I wasn't your typical LA girl. I didn't own designer bags or shoes or sunglasses. I liked funky shit. Purple pants, glass jewelry, fake fur. Those were my style. Red dresses and strappy shoes... not so much.

Renee was out of town, so I ransacked her closet, seeing as her wardrobe was slightly classier than mine. I decided on a low-cut sparkly gold dress because I had a pair of heels that matched perfectly. Luckily, Renee and I were the same size, although she was much taller. It was essentially a mini dress on her, but on me it ended about an inch above my knee. Just long enough to be classy, but just tight enough to be sexy.

Vincent picked me up promptly at 8.30 in a black Maserati. Very close to the black Porsche I'd pictured him in. I felt sexy as I stepped into it. Like a woman. The red lipstick and curls I'd added to my hair also helped me feel closer to his maturity level and less like an intern.

We valeted at the Huntley hotel on Second Street in Santa Monica. I was officially a Hollywood cliché. A cliché in a tight dress and a Maserati, strapped to the arm of someone 20 years my senior. There was a split second where my senses kicked in and I wanted to haul ass in the opposite direction, but instead I kindly kicked my intuition to the curb and followed Vincent to the elevator.

The Penthouse was located on the top floor of the hotel, and was one of the most gorgeous restaurants I'd ever seen. Everything was white. White tables, white chairs, white floors, white walls. They even had white sheer curtains that enveloped each booth; your own private canopy overlooking the city. The bar was lined with candles, and in the corner was a fireplace surrounded by oversized leather chairs.

Vincent and I sat across from each other in one of the cozy booths, and as each drink passed, I wished the curtains weren't sheer so we could have a little privacy. I studied him in his blue-and-white-striped button-up, realizing that I'd forgotten how attractive he was in his absence.

Or maybe it was because I had been a little preoccupied developing a crush on a certain someone…

"Did I tell you how gorgeous you look tonight?" he asked, stroking my hand from across the table.

"Thank you," I said politely.

"I mean it. You look stunning." He removed my hand to grab his menu. "Have you eaten here before?"

I shook my head, taking a sip of champagne. It was my second glass and I was already a little tipsy. Probably because I hadn't eaten lunch.

Tight dress = no lunch. The LA way.

"Oh come on," he teased. "Your other boyfriends must take you to places like this all the time."

Other boyfriends. That was a laugh. I did a quick, mental run-through of all the bad dates I'd been on in LA, and at that moment, the only boyfriend I wanted was him. I stared into his smitten brown eyes, trying to picture us together. Curled up on the couch in his nice home in Beverly Hills. Watching movies and drinking red wine together. Sharing Italian food. It made me feel happy. Safe.

I ordered another glass of champagne and inched closer to him. The booths were U-shaped, and each drink had us slowly gravitating closer to each other. One more drink and I'd be sitting next to him. Two more drinks and I'd be on his lap.

Damn the sheer curtains.

As I sipped my drink, Vincent slid next to me and casually rested his right arm on the back of the booth. His left hand grazed the top

27

of my thigh. My leg tingled.

"You know," he said. "I don't normally do this with coworkers. But there was just something about you…"

Our eyes locked. His hand inched further up my thigh.

"To be honest, I don't get out all that much," he continued. "My son is my whole life. As much as I love my job, I hate all the traveling. Being away from him is really hard."

My heart melted. A good-looking, sweet, devoted dad. He was beyond perfect.

Then why couldn't I get the image of David out of my head?

Stop it, I scolded myself. David is your best friend's boyfriend. You are on a date with a good-looking, single man, who is interested in you. A date you've been looking forward to for a very long time.

I snapped my attention back to Vincent.

"What do you and your son do together?" I asked.

"He plays baseball, so I go to a lot of his games. He loves the movies, too. There's a great theater in the Marina with reclining couches and a full dinner menu. It's his favorite place to go." He smiled proudly.

"That sounds like fun," I said.

"Yeah, I know it's not as exciting as the Hollywood scene, but that's what happens when you're a dad."

I would've taken baseball games and Disney movies over bad dates and pretentious clubs any day.

"Trust me," I assured him. "Hollywood is not all it's cracked up to be."

"Come on. A girl like you?" He looked me up and down. "You must have guys lining up."

"Oh, yeah," I said, mentally sorting through my dating roster. I had them lining up all right. Let's see, there was the Brit whose credit card declined and I got stuck with our two-hundred-dollar bill… the jock who was sleeping with my friend and I simultaneously… the actor who spent our entire date reciting his IMDB page…

"Let's just say the grass is always greener," I said.

Vincent removed his left hand from my thigh and brushed a

loose strand of hair from my face. "Well, do you think any of your boyfriends would mind if I kissed you?" he whispered in my ear.

Before I could answer, his lips were on mine.

It was exactly how I had imagined it. Soft, warm lips, his hand behind my neck. A strong masculine kiss, with a slight sense of aggression. Shivers spreading through my body. The taste of bourbon.

As our lips continued to interlock, I could feel the image of David slipping further and further away.

Vincent pulled back and looked me straight in the eyes. "Well, I hope those boyfriends of yours aren't too jealous, because I might want to do that again."

I giggled. "No boyfriends."

"I find that hard to believe." He looked over my shoulder for a long moment. "But then again, I wouldn't know. I've been out of the dating scene for so long."

I shot him a confused look. "Why? Because of your son?"

"No, because…" He cleared his throat, looking down at the table. "You know. Because I'm married."

If it weren't for the champagne buzz, I'm almost certain I would have clubbed him over the head with the nearest plate and ran for my life.

"You're what?" I asked, positive I hadn't heard him correctly.

"Married," he repeated oh-so-casually. "You knew that."

"You're married." It didn't even come off as a question. More of a dead, lifeless statement.

He nodded, casually taking a sip of his bourbon. As though this was the most normal conversation in the world.

This is not happening, I thought, shutting my eyes tight. Not again.

"Wait, I'm sorry, and how would I have known that?" My voice was rising now.

He shrugged. Mr. Casual. "I just thought you knew."

"Why don't you wear a wedding ring?" The vocal decibels went up another octave. A borderline shriek. I stared accusingly at his bare left hand.

29

He shrugged again. "I stopped wearing it a long time ago."

Just like that. No other explanation. He just "stopped wearing it." You know, because everyone just wakes up one day and decides to stop wearing their wedding ring.

I stared at him, incredulous. Finally, realizing I wasn't going to let it drop, he sighed. "Listen, Justine, people sometimes... grow apart. Relationships change over time. But like I said, I love my son. He's my whole life. So I have to do what I can... for him."

This heartrending speech was interrupted by our waitress, a tall, gorgeous blonde who looked identical to every other waitress in Los Angeles. She smiled at Vincent, clearly admiring the handsome, dark-haired gentleman seated next to me. Only I no longer saw him as handsome. I saw him as a number. Another number to add to the long list of Neanderthals on Justine Sterling's master dating list.

"Are you two ready to order?" she asked.

Vincent looked at me expectantly. This was the moment of truth. He knew that at this moment, one of two things would happen. I would either a) decline dinner and demand to be taken home or b) accept dinner, thus insinuating that I wasn't opposed to his affair proposal. Vincent was a lot of things, but he wasn't an amateur at this game.

Fortunately, neither was I.

"You know," I said, grabbing my menu. "I'm starving. Are you?"

A subtle smile inched across Vincent's lips. He nodded slightly, taking my free hand in his. This was it. I had agreed to dinner. He had me right where he wanted me.

"You order first," I urged him.

I didn't listen to his order. Instead, my eyes browsed the page until I found the most expensive item on the menu.

"And for you, miss?"

I smiled confidently and pointed to the astronomically high-priced beef rib. "I'll have the 32-ounce rib, please. Medium well." I paused, looking over the wine menu. "And actually, I'd like to order a bottle of your finest champagne, too." I turned to Vincent. "Is that okay?"

"Of course," he insisted, waving his hand at the menu. "Whatever you'd like."

I knew he wouldn't object. Even through my alcohol-fogged glasses, I saw him as he really was now. Vincent, with his expensive car, expensive clothes, and expensive home, was a façade. He was an image. On the outside, he had the perfect life. A perfect marriage, a perfect son, and a perfect job that allowed him to travel all over the world. But in reality, he had an unhappy wife, a lonely son, and a job that did nothing but contribute to both of those factors.

And a man like Vincent certainly wouldn't taint his ego and decline a beautiful woman an expensive meal. Especially in front of their beautiful waitress.

I waited for our waitress to bring the champagne bottle, then downed one last glass before excusing myself to the restroom.

"Hurry back," Vincent called after me.

I shot him an award-winning smile before walking away. Luckily, the bar area of the Penthouse was so crowded that it was easy to lose sight of someone.

I snuck around the corner, down the elevator, and hailed a cab home, leaving Vincent all alone with a 32-ounce steak and lots and lots of wasted champagne.

Chapter 6

Renee's house was covered in boxes. She and Dylan had moved into a condo prior to the unexpected pregnancy, so they were now transferring some of their items into storage to make room for the baby. She said they were going to start looking at houses soon.

Renee was sitting upright on the sofa when I walked in, a silver laptop propped on her lap. She was the only person I knew who could wear an oversized t-shirt and a messy ponytail and still look gorgeous.

"I know it's a mess," Renee said, without looking up from her laptop. She looked deeply focused. I felt like I was interrupting something.

"It's fine." I stepped over a box to get to the loveseat. "Do you, um, want me to help you pack?"

"No, it's okay. Dylan will finish at some point." Her eyes were still trained on the computer. Fixated on her latest project, no doubt. Renee was always embarking on some sort of new venture.

I sat quietly on the loveseat and scanned the room while Renee finished typing. The only decorative items that remained were two aromatherapy candles and a black-and-white photo of Renee and Dylan that hung on the wall.

"Sorry. I'm done." Renee slammed her laptop shut like it had offended her with its distraction.

"What are you working on?"

"Oh, it's… nothing." The smile she was hiding indicated otherwise.

"*Renee*." I looked at her accusingly. "Spill."

Her eyes lit up. "Okay, but you can't say anything because Dylan doesn't know yet. Promise?"

I placed my hand over my heart. "Grove's honor."

As we both laughed simultaneously, the mention of our previous joke immediately invoked a flashback in my mind.

It was the fall of 1998, the beginning of our sophomore year. Renee and I were smoking a joint in the Groves, the woods behind our high-school football stadium. We were supposed to be at the football game, according to our parents, but the only reason we'd gone to the game was to stalk our current love interests. After realizing they weren't there, we immediately headed to the Groves.

"Tell me the truth," Renee said, taking a swig from the Budweiser can she'd hidden in her coat pocket. "You did, didn't you?"

"Did what?" I knew exactly what she was referring to.

"You *know*." She rolled her eyes. "Derek. You had sex with him, didn't you?"

I hesitated. Derek Spaulding was the sole reason I'd come to the football game, and the second person I'd ever slept with. But because I was 15 and insecure, I'd hidden this from my friends so they didn't judge me and think I was slutty.

"You can't tell anyone," I insisted. "Especially Beth." Renee's friend, Beth Broadley, was still a virgin and I didn't want to make her feel bad. I also suspected she judged us and thought we were slutty.

Renee placed her hand over her heart. "I swear…" She looked around like she was seeking something sacred to swear on. Coming up empty, she looked back up at me and slurred, "*Grove's* honor."

We laughed like this was the funniest saying ever created.

Much like we're doing now.

"Okay." Renee inched closer to me, something she always did

33

when she was about to dish a secret. Like the close proximity somehow trapped the secret from getting out. "Have you ever heard of Faded? The denim company?"

I nodded.

"Well, they held an online indie artist contest and Electric Wreck was selected as one of their finalists."

"That's great."

Renee shooed me with her hand. "No, what's great is that I just convinced their marketing team to sponsor Electric Wreck's next tour."

I could tell she was waiting for my enthusiastic reaction, but in truth I had no idea what that meant. "So… what happens now?"

"They've agreed to give the band 25 grand to cover their touring expenses. And in exchange, the Faded logo will be on the band's touring vehicle and all their touring flyers and promotional materials."

I had to hand it to her, for someone who had no marketing background whatsoever, the girl certainly had a knack for it. "Renee, that's incredible. Dylan is going to be so excited."

"I know. My little rock star." She smiled nostalgically at the black-and-white photo of them on the wall, then turned to me with a serious expression. "Now, let's talk about the real reason you're here."

The reason? There was a reason I was here? Renee never needed a reason to invite me over.

She inched forward, even closer this time. This was serious. "I'm worried about you," she said in a low voice.

I shot her a confused look. "Worried? Why?"

She rolled her eyes. "*Justine*. We've known each other since we were kids. You think I don't know when something's bothering you?"

Okay, so maybe I hadn't been overly forthcoming about my lingering feelings for David, but come on. He was her ex-boyfriend. It wasn't a favorable subject.

"I'm fine," I insisted. "I'm just having a little trouble adjusting, that's all."

"Well, you don't seem like you're making much of an effort."

I flinched like I'd been slapped. "What's that supposed to mean?"

"It means that you've been home for months, you're not working, you're not attempting to find work, and you're living down in Cape Cod, away from everyone." Renee looked down at the floor nervously. She hated confrontation. "It's like… you're not even trying to adjust. Like you don't want to be here."

"Well, truthfully, I don't." I sighed. "I miss LA. A lot. And I miss…"

"David?"

And there it was, the elephant in the room. Even though Renee and I had made up and moved on, we'd never talked about it. Sure, we'd briefly talked about it, but we'd never *really* talked about it.

"Yeah," I admitted. "I miss him. Every day."

Her face softened. "Why don't you ever mention him?" she asked. "You know I don't care. Not anymore."

"But I care," I said. "And by talking about it, it makes it… real."

Renee placed her right hand on her temple. She looked like half of her felt sorry for me and the other half wanted to kill me. "I don't know why you do this."

"Do what?"

"This." She gestured toward me. "You never tell me how you feel. You keep everything in. You've always done it." She shook her head in frustration. "I don't even know what really happened with you guys. I mean, I know you obviously fell for him pretty hard or else you wouldn't have…" She looked up at me with pleading eyes. "Will you please just talk to me?"

"What do you want to know?"

"Everything. I want to know what happened then, and I want to know what's happening now. I want to know everything."

I took a deep breath and closed my eyes. When I opened them, my best friend was staring at me, silently begging me to let her in.

"Okay," I agreed. "Everything."

I was the saddest girl to ever hold a martini. A walking Sex and the City *episode. Minus the sex.*

I wished Renee was here. If she wasn't home for a funeral, I would've called her for a long-distance cheer-up, but it wasn't the most appropriate time. So instead, I resorted to sitting barefoot on the living-room floor, still wearing Renee's gold dress, crying into a martini glass.

Pathetic, really.

I'm not sure what set it off, because I shouldn't have been this upset. It wasn't like I'd invested much time or energy into my relationship with Vincent. I think this was just the last straw. The end result of the bad-date build-up. I finally thought I'd found someone who was different, and he turned out to be worse than all of them.

At first, it was quite comical. I chuckled to myself in the cab, wondering how long he'd wait at the table, how stupid he'd feel when our waitress realized he'd been ditched. I skipped into my kitchen, made myself a dirty martini, then sat down on my living-room floor and drank.

And somewhere around the second martini, the humor faded.

First, I thought about my parents, and the dreaded question that presented itself every time they called. "So, are you seeing anyone special?" It was the first thing they always asked. Well, technically the third, aside from the traditional "How are you?" and "How's LA?" But the first two were just a buffer to get to the third question, the one they really wanted to ask.

Even worse was their discouraged "oh" after I told them no. I could hear the disappointment echoing from 3,000 miles away. And forget about family parties. My mom would attempt to cover up my patheticness by telling my nosy relatives that I was "kissing a lot of frogs" when they asked about my dating life.

You can only kiss so many frogs before your parents start to think you're a lesbian.

After thinking about it some more, I started to feel bad. It wasn't my parents' fault. I was an only child. I was their only hope for grandchildren.

And then I cried.

I cried because I felt like a huge disappointment. I cried because I was jealous of everyone else's happy relationships. I cried because I was afraid of being alone forever.

The sound at the door made me spill the remains of my drink onto the floor. Shit. I knew Vincent had my address, but I didn't actually think he'd show up here. I was quiet for a minute, hoping he'd go away, but then I watched in horror as the knob turned and the door swung open.

I could have sworn I had locked it behind me when I came in. No, I definitely had. But then how…

"Justine?"

I looked up and locked eyes with David. David in all his six-foot-tall gorgeousness, standing above me with a look of bewilderment on his face. I knew what I looked like. The drunken cry-fest had invoked a black mascara trail under my eyes and a ring of perma-snot under my nose. Not my sexiest moment.

I opened my mouth to explain, fully expecting David to ask what the hell was wrong with me. But instead, to my surprise, he burst out laughing. And it wasn't just a chuckle. The guy was in absolute hysterics.

"Is this what you girls do when guys aren't around?" he asked, trying to catch his breath. "You get dressed up, make martinis and cry? Is there a Lifetime movie marathon on?" He leaned forward and clutched his stomach.

"It's not funny," I said, fighting back a smile. When I thought about what I probably looked like to someone else, it actually was pretty funny. "What are you doing here anyway?"

"I left some stuff here. Renee said I could use the spare key and stop by. She said you wouldn't be here because you were out on a…" A look of recognition came over him as his grin faded. He walked over and sat down next to me on the rug. "I'm guessing the date didn't go well?"

"He's married."

"Ouch. Now I feel bad for laughing." He took my chin in his hand and turned my face toward him. "Although you do look kind of funny having a depressing cocktail party on your floor."

We both burst out laughing.

"I take it Renee didn't tell you I was coming by?" he asked.

I pointed to my phone. I had turned it off so I wouldn't be tempted to answer Vincent's phone calls, wondering where I'd gone. I wanted to make him wait. Make him feel as stupid as I did.

"Do you want to talk about it?" he asked.

I shrugged. "Nothing to talk about, really. He took me out to dinner, kissed me, then proceeded to tell me he was married like it was the most natural thing in the world."

"Hmm, let me guess. Makes a lot of money… drives a flashy car…"

I nodded.

"Typical. So what did you do?"

"Ordered the most expensive bottle of champagne, a 32-ounce steak, then told him I was going to the bathroom and snuck out the back." I grinned proudly.

"Nicely done." David looked like he was impressed. "Well, on that note, I say we go make a few more of these." He took the martini glass from my grasp.

I followed David into the kitchen, happy he'd come to my rescue. This was exactly what Renee would've done. She would've turned the unfortunate situation into a party.

"There's only one problem," I admitted, as David passed me a glass.

"What's that?"

"He's my boss. Does that mean I have to quit?"

"Absolutely not." His tone was so matter-of-fact, like he'd majored

38

in corporate adultery. "Here's what you do. You walk into work on Monday like nothing ever happened. If he tries to bring it up, you casually tell him that you think you should keep your relationship strictly professional." He paused, taking a sip of the martini. His face puckered from the taste, and he took a straight shot from the vodka bottle instead. "The guy isn't going to say shit. If he's your boss, he could lose his job for pulling something like that."

Hmm. He had a point.

"But seriously, though, why the tears?" He cocked his head to the side. "I know I shouldn't be saying this, since you're Renee's best friend and all, but Justine, you're gorgeous. You could have anyone you want. Was this guy really that great?"

I thought back to all the days I had spent with Vincent, joking around in his office, flirting at happy hours. We shared the same sense of humor, I admired his intelligence, and I was crazy attracted to him. He was definitely part of the reason I was upset, but it was more than that.

I was sick of the Vincents of the world. Sick of disappointing my parents. Sick of envying my best friend for having a great guy and wondering if my turn would ever come.

In short, I was lonely.

"I did like him," I said. "I've dated a lot since I moved here, and I really thought that this time it was going to work out."

"LA's a different scene, that's for sure. But, like anywhere, you have to take the good with the bad. On the downside, there are a lot of douches on the dating market. On the upside, it's 75 degrees year-round." His eyes lit up. "Speaking of, I have an idea. You have a pool here, right?"

I nodded. The pool was our apartment's greatest selling point. It was heated, secluded, and open 24 hours.

"I say we go for a swim and exchange worst-date-ever stories." He tossed me a knowing look. "If anything will cheer you up, it's the David Whitman dating rolodex."

I looked down at my outfit hesitantly. After the night I'd had, even the thought of selecting a bikini seemed exhausting. But David's damn puppy eyes and taunting dimples were impossible to resist.

"Fine," I surrendered. "But you'd better have some damn good stories."

The pool was exactly what I needed. The warm water on my skin made my experience with Vincent seem like it was nonexistent. I felt like a kid again.

When I was in the third grade, my father lost his job and we had to live with his parents for a year until he and my mother got back on their feet. While my parents were devastated, I was elated because my grandparents had a giant built-in pool in their backyard.

I always remember that summer being the best of my childhood. My friends from school would come over and we'd swim all day. Sometimes we'd play games ("The Little Mermaid" had made its debut the year prior), and other times we'd just hang out on the blow-up rafts. But I'll never forget the feeling of happiness that came from the water.

That was exactly how I felt right now, swimming around in my pink-and-white-striped bikini. I'd chosen a girl-next-door type of suit, as I didn't want to bust out the thong bikini and give David the wrong idea. David seemed to sense my ease once we started splashing around. He kept looking at me with a proud-dad smile, like he was happy he'd made the suggestion.

The great thing about our pool was its seclusion. It wasn't connected to our apartment building at all. You had to walk through the parking area to get to it, and even then it was fenced in, so you couldn't see in from the outside. Luckily, our apartment management was very low-key and didn't close it at a certain time. The glowing blue pool lights stayed on all night, unlike a lot of other buildings that closed the swim area at ten.

"Okay," David said, resting his arm on the ledge. "Worst date ever. Go."

I had to pick just one? This could take a while…

"I met a guy at the W hotel last year, who introduced himself as D.X.X." I used hand quotations as I said the acronym. "I refused to call him this idiotic term, but he insisted it was his name."

David was already laughing. "Don't you love how no one in Hollywood uses their real name? It's like, if they tell people their name is John Smith, they're destined for career failure."

"Yeah, well, he was cute, and I was drunk, so I agreed to go out with him." I sighed, partly wishing I hadn't agreed to divulge this horribly embarrassing story to a gorgeous guy. "I met him at Katana, that sushi place on Sunset, the next night and he tells me that if I want to have a few drinks, I can stay at his place since he lives right next door. He promised to be a perfect gentleman."

"Famous last words," David joked.

"Well he was, at first. We both fell asleep shortly after we got to his house. But then I woke up in the middle of the night because I heard a weird noise and I look over, and the guy is kneeling above me on the bed, jerking himself off."

"While you were sleeping?" David threw his head back and laughed loudly. "That's got to be illegal somehow."

I lowered my head, mortified.

He waved his hands in front of him like he was surrendering. "Okay, I'm starting to understand the martini pity-party." He swam closer to me. "I went home with a girl once, after our first date. We were taking our clothes off, having a good time, and then she tells me that I don't have to use a condom. Because she's already pregnant."

I was feeling better already.

"I went out with an actor once," I said. "And I asked him what he did when he wasn't shooting. He started running his hands over his body and said 'well, not to be cheesy, but my job is to maintain this'."

"Stop it."

"That wasn't even the bad part. The bad part was that my gorgeous classmate showed up at the same restaurant we were at, and he immediately dropped the douche act and invited her to join us. He ignored me for the rest of the dinner and stared at her fake boobs the entire time."

"So how was the second date?"

"Funny."

David grinned. "I went out with an actress once, too. The date was awesome, actually, until her fiancé showed up at the restaurant and punched me in the jaw."

"You're lying."

He pointed to a small scar on his chin. "I don't date actresses anymore."

Okay, I was really starting to feel better. If a hot catch like David had just as bad of a track record as I did, then maybe there wasn't something wrong with me.

David paddled in a circle around me, then lifted me up and tossed me underwater. After I came back up and wiped my face, he pulled me towards him.

"Well, Justine, I have good news and bad news," he announced, looking into my eyes ever-so-seriously. "The bad news is that I officially made the worst martini ever, therefore I'm not in the best shape to drive home." His lips twitched devilishly. "The good news is that I promise to be a perfect gentleman."

Chapter 7

Renee had decided to start house-hunting. I think it was partially because she couldn't stand living in a cramped condo filled with boxes, and partially because she needed a new project to work on. Renee couldn't sit still. She loved writing, and when she wasn't working on a freelance assignment, she was managing Dylan's band. And when she wasn't managing Dylan's band, she was searching for somewhere else to direct her energy.

Today, she'd decided to focus her energy on houses. Dylan was at rehearsal and wasn't sure if he'd be able to make it in time, so she'd elected me to be her co-conspirator for the afternoon.

I agreed to meet her at a new real-estate company in the city. Apparently they were headquartered in New York but had recently opened a Boston location. A friend of Renee's had referred them, so she'd made an appointment to go in and meet with one of the agents. I couldn't think of a less fun way to spend the afternoon, but Dylan had promised to meet us after his rehearsal, so I hoped I'd be off the hook soon enough.

The Keller office was bright and beautiful. Everything seemed to be made of glass or granite: a vibrant, open space. The receptionist looked up from her computer as I walked in.

"Welcome to Keller Realty," she greeted. "Do you have an appointment with us today?"

I pointed to Renee, who was already seated in the lobby, filling out paperwork. "I'm with her," I said. Renee smiled and waved me over.

I strolled across the office and sat down next to Renee, still admiring the surroundings.

"Nice office, huh?" Renee asked, following my gaze.

I nodded. "Have you been here long?"

"No. I'm just filling out some papers." She looked down guiltily and picked up another clipboard from the table next to her. "But there's another reason I picked this place."

I eyed her suspiciously. "Why do I feel like this has to do with me?"

She bit her lip. "Well, they also specialize in rentals. So I thought maybe… you could look at apartments, too. Wouldn't it be fun if we both looked at places together?"

I sighed. Ever since I'd started dishing the David details, Renee seemed gung-ho on helping me move my life forward. Which was sweet. I just didn't know if I was ready for it yet.

"Renee, they're not going to rent to someone who's unemployed."

"I know. But maybe if you see a place you really like, it'll motivate you to start looking." She pouted. "Besides, I hate that you live so far away."

"It's only an hour…"

"Well it'll be longer in a few months with summer Cape traffic." She pushed the clipboard closer to me. "Please?"

I rolled my eyes and reluctantly took the clipboard from her. "Fine, I'll fill it out. But I don't know if I want to live in the city. Too much traffic."

"They have places all over the south shore."

Of course they did. I appreciated her efforts to cheer me up, but I highly doubted that looking at apartments out of my price range was going to heal my broken heart.

"It'll be fun," she insisted, sensing my hesitation. "You can just look at some different places and neighborhoods. Get a feel for what you like."

"Okay, okay," I said, accepting defeat. "I'll do it."

"Ms. Evans?" The receptionist walked over to us. "Have you finished?"

Renee nodded and handed her the clipboard of papers. The receptionist looked down at Renee's protruding stomach, beaming.

"So, how far along are you?" she asked, clasping her hands together.

"Six months," Renee answered.

"Do you know if it's a boy or a girl?"

Renee shook her head. "It's going to be a surprise. My fiancé doesn't want to know."

"Oh, that's great. Congratulations." She returned to her desk, then glanced over her shoulder in our direction. "Mr. Keller should be with you in a few minutes."

"Mr. Keller, huh?" I turned to face Renee. "Is the President himself giving you a housing tour?"

"His son," the receptionist corrected. "He's in from New York to help set up the new office. But trust me, you're in good hands." She winked at Renee.

Renee leaned closer to me. "Do you think it's weird that Dylan wants the baby's sex to be a surprise?"

I shrugged. "Some people like surprises. Why?"

"Because it's killing me," she whispered. "I've thought about finding out and just not telling him."

"Don't," I warned. Renee couldn't keep anything to herself.

"I know. I won't. I just *really* want to."

"What do you think it is?"

She placed her right hand on her stomach and looked down. "I think it's a boy. I've read that boys carry low."

It was still so strange to me, seeing my best friend as a mother, hearing her use big-girl words like "fiancé." It was like we had grown up overnight. I still pictured us as the girls who skipped class to smoke pot in the woods.

"Renee Evans?"

Oh, my. Well *hello* Mr. Keller. I had to assume it was Mr. Keller by the way he carried himself. He walked like he owned the place. And he looked like... wow. His face was perfectly chiseled, his body rock hard, his skin tanned and smooth, his eyes a nearly impossible shade of brown. I had never seen eyes like his. They were so light they were almost gold.

"Oh my God!" Renee's scream rung through the entire office. By the time I looked over at her, she was already out of her seat, barreling towards him.

"I can't believe it!" Renee threw her arms around him in a tight hug, then took a step back, studying him. "Walter, what are you doing here?"

Walter? How did I know that name? It sounded oddly familiar...

"Oh, *fuck* no!" I heard a loud yell from behind me, and turned around to find Dylan storming through the office, decked out in an all-leather ensemble. "No way! Absolutely not!"

Renee turned around and grabbed Dylan's hand, pulling him closer. "Walter, I'm sure you remember Dylan."

"Ah, yes, Dylan. Of course." He flashed Dylan and Renee a charming smile. God, even his teeth were flawless. "So I see the two of you worked things out?"

"We did." Renee glanced down at her stomach.

"Are you kidding me, Renee?" Dylan eyes were aflame. I'd never seen him so mad. Everyone in the office was starting to stare. "How could you not tell me this?"

"Relax," Renee said in her calmest voice. "I had no idea this was his office until just now." She turned to face Walter. "Are you living in Boston now?"

"No, I'm just here for a few weeks. My dad wanted to branch out and open an office here, so I'm helping him get everything up and running."

Suddenly, Renee whipped around, remembering I was there. "Justine!" she called, motioning for me to come over and break the tension. I rose from my seat. "This is…"

"Walter," I interrupted. "So I heard." I extended my hand. "Justine Sterling."

"Walter Keller," he said, shaking it. "A pleasure."

Is it ever, I thought. Who the hell was this guy? And why was Dylan so pissed?

"So, are we still going to…" Walter looked hesitantly between Renee and Dylan. "I mean, if you guys would prefer to use another agency, I completely understand."

Dylan started to say something, but Renee silenced him. A slow smirk emerged on her face as she looked back at me. "Actually, Justine is looking for a new apartment." She feigned an innocent expression. "Maybe the two of you should get started on that while Dylan and I discuss our options?"

"Sure," Walter agreed, turning to face me. "Why don't we go into my office and discuss the locations and price ranges you're thinking of, and then we can see what's available?"

I looked at Renee. Grinning like the little shit she was. But hell, if anything was going to help me get over David, Walter Keller was a good start.

Los Angeles, CA
April 2009

I didn't sleep with David that night. I mean, sure, I slept with him, but not in the sexual sense. Only in the nocturnal sense.

After changing out of our soaking-wet swimsuits, David and I somehow ended up in my bed. I'm not really sure how it happened. One minute, I was curled up under my covers, trying to warm up because my hair was soaking wet. The next minute, David was sitting on the edge of my bed, attempting to continue our conversation. Eventually, we both fell asleep without leaving that general proximity.

By the time I woke up the next morning, David was no longer in my bed, so it sort of felt like it never happened. Instead, he was now in the kitchen, making coffee and eggs and toast. God, he was so damn perfect. Even in his gym shorts with messy bedhead. I remember, at that distinct moment, thinking about how much I wished I could find someone like him. And hating Renee for not realizing how lucky she was.

"So, little lady," David said, placing two plates of food down on the kitchen table. "What are your plans for this evening?"

I sat down at the table and rubbed my throbbing temples. "Well, I can tell you what I won't be doing."

"Hmm... breaking up more families?"

I glared at him. He grinned.

"Too soon?"

I picked a piece of crust off my toast and threw it at him. "Funny," I retorted. "I think I'm just going to stay in tonight."

He took a bite of scrambled eggs and nodded. "Well, if you're here later, maybe I'll swing by. I don't really feel like going out either."

There was a part of me that felt like I should say no, because it felt wrong to be spending time with Renee's boyfriend when she wasn't there. But there was also a part of me that thought I was overreacting. I mean, what was the big deal? We hadn't done anything wrong. We had a drink, went swimming, and fell asleep. That was it.

So why did I feel guilty?

Deep down, I knew why. It was because of the way I felt about him. The way I'd felt about him since the moment I met him. But of course, I couldn't tell him that.

"That's fine," I said. "As long as it's cool with Renee."

"I'm sure she'd be happy that I was here to cheer you up. Since she couldn't be."

It was then that I saw something in his eyes. That look. It was the same look I always fought to ignore, but it seemed more intense now, more dangerous. Maybe because we were alone. Or maybe because my feelings for him weren't entirely one-sided. But I could've sworn, at that moment, that I felt something between us change.

48

Just after eight o'clock that night, David strolled through my door carrying a pizza and a giant paper bag. I hated admitting it to myself, but I was secretly hoping he'd come. Not just because he was fun and funny and good company, but it was nice having a guy around. I hadn't been in a serious relationship in years, and I missed it. I missed the company. Renee was the best friend I could ever ask for, but sometimes I liked having someone of the opposite sex to watch a movie with. Someone to tell me I'm pretty, make me feel good. Maybe flirt with me a little.

I know, I know. Loneliness was no excuse to be a lousy friend.

"Okay, so I got half cheese, half pepperoni," David announced, placing the pizza down on the coffee table. "I also grabbed a bottle of soda and every chick flick known to woman." He emptied the remains of the paper bag onto the table, waving his hands over the pile like he was demonstrating a sacred display.

I picked up the stack of DVDs. Pretty Woman, The Notebook *and* Clueless. *I burst out laughing.*

"Seriously?"

"The lady at the store said Dirty Dancing *was the ultimate pick, but I didn't think I'd be able to sit through it."*

Aw. Not only was he gorgeous and charming, but he was thoughtful too.

I hated Renee.

"Well, lucky for you, I think I'm the only female alive who hates that movie." I reached out and handed one to him. "I'm voting for Clueless."

And for the next two hours, we consumed lots of pizza and watched Alicia Silverstone roam the streets of Beverly Hills.

And somewhere around the end of the movie, we stopped paying attention to it.

"Did you tell Renee you were coming over?" I heard myself ask. Truthfully, I was having so much fun that I didn't want to bring her up. I wanted to pretend that David and I were in our own little world together. That was, unfortunately, the problem. I was starting

to forget her, and I needed to bring reality back.

"Yeah. I talked to her earlier."

I waited for something more, but nothing came. "So, she's cool with you hanging out here while she's gone?"

David nodded absently. He seemed like something was on his mind.

"Hey." I nudged him. "Are you okay?"

Finally, he made eye contact with me. "It's just that... to be honest, she seemed like she couldn't have cared less. I don't know how to describe it, but she's been different lately. Really different. I think..." His eyes went straight to the floor. "I think she's going to break up with me."

Shit, I thought. He knows. Shit, shit, shit.

"Really?" I asked, attempting a surprised expression. "Why do you think that?"

David's lips curled up. "Renee was right," he said. "You are a terrible liar."

Shit, shit, shit, shit, shit.

"She told you, didn't she?"

"No," I said, a little too quickly. "I mean, she might've mentioned..."

"Forget it," he said, putting up his hand to stop me. "I'm not going to put you in the middle. I can sense when something's different. I just feel like... nothing's ever good enough for her. She wants this perfect guy who's the exact mold of herself, someone who likes all the same music and reads all the same books, and let's face it." He motioned to his outfit – blue baseball hat, clean polo shirt, white running sneakers. "That's not me."

My thoughts exactly, I thought.

"Remember how you told me last night that I was stupid to cry over Vincent, because I could have anyone I wanted?" I asked him. "Well, the same thing goes for you. You're..."

Oh, no. Here it comes.

"You're perfect," I blurted out. "And I love Renee to death, but if she doesn't see that, then she's crazy."

"Perfect, huh?" He placed both of his hands over his heart. "Well,

I think I was wrong about you, Justine. You actually are a good liar."

"I'm serious! That's exactly what I thought when she told me she was thinking of br…"

I clasped both hands over my mouth.

Shiiiiit.

Renee was going to kill me.

"I knew it!" David yelled. To my surprise, he was grinning. He didn't exactly seem to be taking the news to heart. "It's okay. I won't say anything. I knew it anyway."

"Sorry. I guess that was the…" I looked around for something to blame my big mouth on. Soda talking."

David raised his eyebrows, then reached over and poured the remains of the Coke bottle into my glass. "Well if that's the soda talking, then what are we going to do when we run out?"

Chapter 8

Walter Keller was exactly what you visualized when you imagined the perfect man. Handsome with a boy-next-door wholesomeness. Polite with sincerity. Successful without the slightest trace of arrogance. The movie character you never actually met in real life.

I mean, let's face it. In reality, Richard Gere doesn't marry the prostitute. He gets his $200-dollar blowjob and goes home. No one actually meets a real-life Richard Gere.

Walter and I had been cruising the south shore all afternoon looking at apartments, but my focus had been more on him than my future place of abode. Despite his perfections, I couldn't dig up one ounce of attraction to him. It was like David had taken up permanent residency in my heart, and everyone else paled in comparison.

Would I ever feel that way again?

"The cabinets need to be replaced," Walter said, gesturing around the kitchen of another apartment. It was the third one we'd looked at so far, and fortunately Renee had been right. The thought of a new apartment was exciting. A new home, a fresh start – it was exactly what I needed.

"The bathroom was just renovated," Walter continued, leading me to a bathroom with glass shower doors and beige rock tile.

"This is nice," I said, looking around. You could tell everything was new, even the sink. I imagined myself soaping up in the gorgeous shower.

"Yeah, once they finish painting the living room and replace the kitchen cabinets, it should be good to go." Walter led me back to the living room, which had an open kitchen and hardwood floors, another selling point. "So, what do you think so far?"

"This one is my favorite," I said, which was true. The others were okay, just a little smaller and more outdated. "But like I mentioned, I don't have a full-time job yet."

"That's okay," he assured me. "The place still needs some work, so it won't be ready for a while. And we have some other units opening up in the building that are identical to this one."

I followed Walter out the front door, but before we reached his car, he turned around to face me. "You know, there's a great café right around the corner. Do you want to grab some lunch before we head back to the office?"

I considered. "Sure," I agreed. "That sounds great."

The Seasons Café was a little hole in the wall that reminded me of my grandmother's kitchen. The walls were painted bright yellow, and each table and chair set were mismatched, like they'd been randomly selected from yard sales and antique stores. I went over each menu item a dozen times before settling on fruit salad. I wasn't all that hungry, but I didn't want Walter to eat alone.

"So," Walter said, sitting down across from me. "You're one of those girls, huh?"

I shot him a confused look.

He pointed to my plate. "This place has the best food around and all you're going to have is fruit?"

"I happen to like fruit," I said in a jokingly defensive tone.

Walter laughed. He looked like a little kid when he smiled, innocent with a trace of mischief. "Ah, yes. You California natives are known to be pretty health-conscious, right?"

I stuck my fork into a strawberry. "Well, I wouldn't call myself a native. I only went to college there."

I paused, wondering if now was the right time to ask him about what had happened at the office. He'd been so professional all day, it had seemed kind of inappropriate to stray from the subject of housing. But lunch seemed more fitting for casual conversation.

"So, how do you know Renee?" I asked him.

"She didn't tell you?"

I shook my head. "Your name sounds familiar, but I can't remember why."

He hesitated for a moment, taking a bite of his sandwich. I couldn't tell if it was chicken or tuna salad, but it looked good. I was beginning to regret my fruit decision.

"I met Renee in New York," he answered. "Dylan's band was playing at the same benefit concert that my brother's band was playing."

"Your brother is in a band?" I looked at him skeptically. He seemed so proper and well-rounded, with his gray suit and chivalrous manners. I imagined him to come from a preppy, white-collar kind of family.

"Yeah, he's definitely not a typical Keller," he joked. "The rest of us don't have a musical bone in our bodies, but he loves it. He was top of his class at Berklee." He shook his head, like he was digressing. "Anyway, after the show, Renee and Dylan got into an argument, so she and I went to grab something to eat."

Now I remembered. Renee had told me all about that night, and about Walter. That was the night that she and Dylan finally admitted they had feelings for each other. And Walter was indirectly the cause, because Dylan was jealous and pissed off that Renee left the show with him, which had forced him to tell her how he really felt.

"To be honest," he continued. "I really liked her and wanted to keep in touch, but I knew there was something going on between them. I didn't want to interfere."

Of course. Yet another perfect guy that Renee could've had. I loved her, I really did, but sometimes I couldn't help but feel like life had handed her a better deal.

Sensing my distraction, Walter waved his hand in front of my face. "Something I said?" he asked.

"No. I just remembered that Renee had told me that story a while ago." I forced a smile. "She always finds the good ones."

Walter cocked his head to the side. "Why do you say that?"

I shrugged. "She just always seems to meet a lot of great guys. I don't have much luck in that department."

"You know, I used to feel the same way," he said. "When I met Renee, I had all but given up on dating. I was the stereotypical 'nice guy' and girls always left me for… well, honestly, for guys like Dylan."

Walter and I broke into laughter, because we both knew it was true. Women rarely fell for the nice guys. I was guiltier of it than anyone.

"Luckily, shortly after I met Renee, I met my girlfriend," Walter continued. "It was great because I felt like I'd finally found someone who appreciated me for who I was. A lot of women like the bad-boy types, but that's just not who I am."

I nodded sympathetically. "I left LA because my ex-boyfriend broke up with me," I confessed. "And what you just described… about not finding anyone who appreciates you… that's exactly how I feel." I shut my eyes tight. "And the reason I haven't found an apartment or a full-time position, is because I haven't been looking. I guess I was hoping that eventually he'd call me and want me to move back. I thought that maybe, after some time, he'd realize he made a mistake. Because I can't imagine feeling this way about him if he doesn't feel it back. But…"

"But he hasn't," Walter finished.

I shook my head. I wanted to cry. I was so pathetic. But when I looked up at Walter, he made me feel better because he didn't look judgmental at all. He looked caring and wholesome and smiled like the cutest little boy I'd ever seen, and he looked like someone who would never in a million years hurt anyone. He gave me faith in men, at a time when all I wanted was some asshole who wasn't caring and smiled like he was up to something and hurt people on a daily basis and probably didn't feel the least bit bad about it.

"Well, if he hasn't called, and he didn't chase you out here, then he's not for you," Walter said simply. "Trust me, I know it doesn't feel like it now, because right now you think he's the only one for you and you can't imagine ever feeling this way about anyone again. We've all been there. And when you're going through it, there's nothing anyone can say or do to make it better. You wake up every day and everything sucks." He grinned again. The little-boy grin. "But then one day, you wake up and the sun shines again. You start to feel like yourself again. And when you actually meet the person you're supposed to be with, you'll thank God you didn't end up with someone who didn't appreciate you for who you really are."

Los Angeles, CA
April 2009

I didn't sleep at all that night. Neither did David. The conversation between us just seemed to unravel and expand into further levels of depth, and before I knew it, the sun was streaming through the window.

I told him things I had never told anyone. My fears, my insecurities. He was the only person I had ever felt completely, wholeheartedly comfortable with. It was like I could be myself, unconditionally, without judgment. It felt real. It felt right.

David propped his head up on his elbow and stared at me from the other end of the sofa. "You do know you're beautiful, right?" David, who typically joked about everything, was being completely serious.

I thought about it. Sure, guys usually told me that I looked like Denise Richards when they were hitting on me, because I was petite and had the long, brown hair, big, blue eyes, and little nose to match.

56

I didn't think I was unattractive, but in a land filled with models and actresses, I didn't think I necessarily stood out either.

"Everyone in LA is beautiful," I said.

"Yeah, but you have an edge. You have that feisty east-coast attitude. And honestly…" He hesitated, clearing his throat. "If we weren't in these circumstances, I'd be with you in a heartbeat."

"Oh come on, Renee's great," I said, trying to bring my best friend back into the picture before I forgot about her altogether and did something stupid.

"She is. But she can be really critical. I bet you'd watch football with me on a Sunday and not roll your eyes."

I would've done anything with him if it meant I could stare into those crazy brown eyes for one more second.

"I'm really glad I came over tonight," he said in a low voice, changing the subject. "I can't tell you the last time I felt…" He closed his eyes. "I shouldn't be saying this."

He shouldn't have. But I wanted him to.

There was a pause and neither of us said anything. Something was changing. I could feel it. It was like an unstoppable force was pulling us together.

When I looked up, his eyes locked with mine, and my heart stopped. The look on his face was unfamiliar to me. He was usually so laid back and funny, but the intensity in his eyes felt like he was an entirely different person.

He inched his body closer and pressed his face toward mine, but I pulled back.

"David, I can't," I said. "Trust me, I'd love to, but…"

"But what?"

"But you're my best friend's boyfriend! Did you forget that?"

In an instant, David was back. His eyes went wide as he broke into a fit of laughter. "She's going to break up with me anyway! She can't be that mad if she doesn't even want to be with me."

His laugh was contagious. He made a serious situation seem harmless. I loved that about him; his easygoing nature. Women tended to overthink, overanalyze, and overdramatize everything, and David lived in a world where everything was fine. Always.

"Don't you feel this, between us?" he asked. "I know you feel it. I've felt it since the minute we met."

"Of course I feel it," I admitted. "But I love Rene, and I would never do that to her."

"Okay, then we'll wait," he said. "We'll wait until she breaks up with me. We'll wait until she moves on. But… there's something here Justine. You can't argue that." He looked straight into my eyes again. "Maybe we can't act on it now, but someday."

And then, as the sun came pouring through the window, I drifted off to sleep next to him.

Someday. I could live with that.

Chapter 9

I read once that candid photos were like time machines because they allowed you to pause time and enjoy the smallest and most genuine details of any given moment in life. They didn't include fake smiles or premeditated poses; they were real. They captured sincere emotions and expressions, ones that were often overlooked because they happened so quickly. Everyday interactions occurred so frequently and so fast, it was easy to miss them.

But sometimes, it was necessary to pause a specific moment in your life in order to understand it. To see it more clearly.

I knew there was something I was missing. Some clear explanation as to what went wrong. But as I looked down at the piece of evidence in my hand, all I saw were two people enjoying each other's company. Smiling. Happy. In love.

I had finally removed it from its hiding place. My favorite photo of us. My Sphinx coworker, Jasmine, had taken the picture without our knowledge, while we were at a work event. David's arm was draped casually around my shoulder, his eyes searching for mine. My head was tilted down, my eyes closed, both of us laughing in unison. We looked so natural, so at ease with each other.

I had gone over it in my head, again and again, but it still didn't make sense. We *were* happy. We *were* those two people in the picture. Two people who, at one time, couldn't live without each other.

As hard as I stared at the photo, searching for some sort of clue, something on David's face to indicate his mind was elsewhere, I couldn't find anything. The image of him in the photo was the same image stored in my mind. An image of a man whose full attention was on me. A man who loved me.

Fortunately, I had learned a lot from my conversation with Walter. David may have been in love with me at one time, but he wasn't anymore. That part of my life was over. There was, however, someone out there who would someday love me for who I was, and as much as I hated to admit it, that person wasn't David.

Now if only I could get myself to believe it.

Walter's words had been echoing in my head for days. *If he hasn't called, and he didn't chase you out here, then he's not for you.*

He was right. I was holding onto something that wasn't there. Wasting all my energy on someone who wasn't worth it.

I took one last look at the picture, then stuffed it back into the box where I'd been keeping it.

And just then, something inside of me clicked.

There was something that photo had told me, but it had nothing to do with how David felt about me. It had to do with how *I* felt about me. Ever since I could remember, photography had been my one true love, my passion. I had taken endless photos of my adventures growing up with Renee, and every year I gave her an album or a scrapbook for Christmas. Not because she necessarily wanted the photos, but because I loved them. I loved developing them, editing them, piecing them together. They told a story. They meant something to me.

I had originally retrieved the photo with the intention of studying David, to try to discern some hidden answer, a facial expression, some body language I'd overlooked. Something that was off. But instead, I found myself studying the actual photo. The lighting, the background, the intricate details. It was then that I realized I'd found my answer.

I'd lost myself. I'd given up my passion and my entire sense of purpose without even realizing it. I had put love first, put *him* first, and ultimately lost both of us in the process.

I thought back to the night that David and I had discussed LA, and what separated me from every other girl in the city. I didn't realize it at the time, but I did now. It wasn't my looks, or my "east-coast edge" as David suggested. My edge was my sense of purpose. My passion, my ambition – that was what really separated me from everyone else. That was what separated everyone.

And with that, I picked up my laptop and opened the classified ads page. This was it. I was moving forward with my life. I wouldn't waste another day on some guy who didn't care about me. And honestly, how could I expect him to? Not only had I not loved myself, I'd forgotten who I was altogether. Given myself up completely for a man.

Therapists would have a field day with me.

Los Angeles, CA
April 2009

We had spent the entire day on Sunday together. We ate chips and salsa and watched football, while David educated me on kick-offs, fumbles, handoffs, passing plays, and defensive plays. I didn't care about any of them. I was just watching the clock, dreading the hours until our weekend of fun came to an unwanted halt.

He left Sunday night. I asked him to, even though I didn't really want him to. Neither of us wanted the weekend to end. But it was the right thing to do. Renee would be home in a week, and prolonging the inevitable would only make it harder.

By the time Monday morning came, I had completely forgotten about Vincent. Friday night seemed like a lifetime ago. But as I strolled through Sphinx's hallway towards the marketing department, a growing pit began to form in my stomach.

Just as I turned the corner, there he was. All six foot two inches of lying, cheating, married boss scum. Casually standing in his office doorway, scrolling through his Blackberry. It's funny how quickly our perceptions of people can change. Last week, I would have drooled over his carved biceps, waited for his eyes to give my tight gray sweater a once-over. Now I just wondered if he was texting his wife another lie about where he was going to be later.

Then came the moment I dreaded. I attempted to tip-toe quietly to my desk, but before I turned the corner, his gaze found me. Our eyes connected for a brief moment before I looked away and bolted to my seat. My heart was pounding. Sure, the thought of a dateless Vincent surrounded by a bunch of expensive plates had seemed amusing on Friday, while David and I clinked martini glasses together, but now, not so much. The fact that my job was on the line kind of sucked the humor out of it.

I turned on my computer and waited impatiently for it to warm up, silently hoping I'd have some imperative email that would save me from him. An emergency intern meeting. A Monday-morning fire drill. Something.

No such luck. I could feel him hovering over my desk, but I refused to look up. Instead, my eyes remained on the screen in front of me as I pretended it wasn't completely blank. I practiced my best perplexed facial expression, the one I always used when trying to avoid someone. I narrowed my eyes, crinkled my eyebrows together, and tried to look really engrossed in something, like my computer was broken and I was desperately trying to find the solution. I hoped my expression would read, "Sorry Vincent, but I'm just so busy right now that I don't have time to look up and see your disgusting married face. Oh, and by the way, how was that steak?"

"Good morning, Justine." Ugh. Even the sound of his voice made my skin crawl. I couldn't believe that a few days ago, I'd found it sexy. Now it just slithered into the middle of the room like a snake.

"Good morning, Vincent," I said coldly. My eyes were still on the computer. Luckily, it had finally come to life and prompted me for my password, so I was able to avoid eye contact for another ten seconds as I slowly typed it in.

He waited for me to look up. And waited. Finally, realizing he wasn't going anywhere, I looked at him. He eyed me warily, a faint sneer on his face. It was as if he was saying, "Two can play at this game."

"May I see you in my office for a moment?" Ever so polite, that Vincent. Such proper manners.

Without a word, I stood up and followed him to his office. Inside, everything was still in the same place as when I'd last seen it – leather couches propped against the back wall, giant glass windows overlooking the city – but it felt different. It didn't feel like the warm place where we'd escaped every day, laughing over coffee while Vincent filled me in on office gossip. It felt cold. Dirty. Like a prison.

"That was quite the stunt you pulled on Friday," he said, shutting the door behind him. I watched as he crossed the office and took a seat at his desk, the sneer reappearing. "You know, if you wanted to leave, you could've just said so."

"Oh, but where's the fun in that?" I asked sweetly.

He leaned back in his chair and folded his arms, looking as though he was unsure of how to respond. I took a deep breath, remembering David's advice.

"Listen," I said. "Given the circumstances, I think we should just keep our relationship professional from now on."

"Oh, but where's the fun in that?"

I wanted to slap the shit-eating grin off his face. Clearly, he thought there was still a small chance of victory. That I'd had my fun, gotten my revenge, and we were even now. But there was no way I'd be able to resist his Italian charm forever. Someday, I'd reconsider. I'd cave.

Luckily, the next chess move was mine.

"You're right," I said ever-so-seductively, inching closer to him. I clasped my hands together and rested my elbows on my knees, allowing him a clear view of the cleavage lingering beneath my gray v-neck sweater. "That wouldn't be much fun, would it?"

He shook his head as the devilish look in his eyes grew.

"But actually," I said, pulling myself upright. I put on my best perplexed look again, pretending to consider my options. "I think a custody battle would be far less fun, though. Don't you?"

He didn't say anything. He didn't have to. I watched his eyes darken, and took that as my cue to exit.

"I'll see you at two o'clock to go over the new ad campaign," I called to him. Then I shut the door behind me.

For the rest of the day, all I could think about David. I wanted so badly to tell him about Vincent. I wanted to toast martinis with him in my kitchen and see his eyes light up and watch him laugh uncontrollably. I wanted him to curl up on my couch with me and remind me that there were a million non-Vincents in the world who would be lucky to have me.

Basically, in a span of three days, I had become attached to the one guy in the world I shouldn't be.

I began typing on my computer, hoping to distract myself. Yes, I'd had a fun weekend with David, and yes, I wished we'd met under different circumstances, but we hadn't. He belonged to my best friend and as much as he made me weak in the knees, I had to respect that. I couldn't keep falling for the wrong guys. It was like an endless cycle of unavailable men that I had on rotation. Somewhere out there was a nice, single guy for me. I just had to keep swimming through the dating pool until I found him.

I looked at the clock. It was almost five. I had one more task to finish up for the day and then I was free to go.

Sphinx was looking to hire additional producers for their upcoming game, so our HR department had assigned me the task of posting the job advertisement on our company social media pages to get the word out. Just as I was posting the link, my desk phone rang.

"Hi, Cheryl," I said, looking down at the caller ID. Cheryl, our resident receptionist, was a curvy, cheery black woman who had worked at Sphinx for almost ten years.

"Hi little Miss Thang," she said cheerfully. This was the nickname she had given me. I had no idea why. Probably because I was the only female at Sphinx who didn't wear sneakers. "Can you come out to the lobby?"

Uh oh. I immediately envisioned Vincent waiting in the lobby for me, then escorting me to a vacant conference room with my termination papers.

"Um, yeah," I stammered. "Is everything okay?"

"Girl, everything's fine!" she yelled into the phone. Then she lowered her voice to a whisper. "You have a visitor."

A visitor? Shit. My next mental image was of Vincent's wife adjusting her blonde curls and designer clothes in the lobby while she waited to attack the intern her husband was after. I had no idea what she really looked like, but I assumed a blonde trophy wife was fairly accurate.

"What kind of visitor?" I whispered back.

"Miss Thang, get your little butt out here and you'll see!" Then she hung up.

I finished posting the advertisements, shut my computer down, and grabbed my purse. I tried not to panic as I headed towards the lobby.

But when I rounded the corner, I couldn't believe my eyes.

Standing in the middle of the lobby, wearing a black t-shirt, distressed jeans, and a mile-wide grin, was David. David, looking happy and carefree as usual. Just seeing him made me forget everything that had happened with Vincent, and my entire tedious workday altogether. He was like a breath of clean air.

"David?" I asked, wide-eyed. "What are you doing here?"

"Well, I was…"

And as luck would have it, before he could finish his sentence, Vincent came strolling through the lobby. His smooth stride slowed as he looked back and forth from David to me, then back to David.

"Hi, Vincent," I said with fake enthusiasm. I watched David's eyes widen, which was exactly why I'd done it. I knew he'd pick up on it.

"So this is the infamous Vincent," David exclaimed, turning to shake Vincent's hand. "David Whitman. Justine has told me so much *about you."*

The look Vincent gave him could've killed small children. He reached out and reluctantly shook David's hand. "Justine has been a great help here," said Mr. Professional. The tone in his voice was about as flat as his expression.

"What are you doing here?" I asked again, turning back to David.

"Just thought I'd show up and surprise my girl."

Without another word, Vincent disappeared into the hallway. David looked as though it took everything he had not to burst into hysterics.

"Okay, seriously," I said, lowering my voice. "What are you really doing here?"

"Well, I was going to go home after work," he said. "But then I started thinking about how much fun I had this weekend. And I remembered that one of my favorite restaurants is right down the street from here. So, I thought, if you don't have plans tonight…"

I grabbed his arm and led him towards the elevator. "Let's go."

"Yeah?" He looked surprised that I'd agreed.

Yes, you idiot, I thought to myself. I haven't stopped thinking about you all damn day.

"Bye, Cheryl!" I yelled over my shoulder.

Cheryl gave me her "mom look" as I called it, where she peered over her glasses and shook her head knowingly.

"Looks like somebody's in love," she called after me.

Chapter 10

Day number four of the job-hunt. I had submitted my résumé to at least ten different positions and had yet to hear back. So far every position I'd applied for was almost identical to my position at Sphinx. Digital media coordinators, social media managers, online marketing reps, they were all the same. Which was fine, because it was really the only relevant experience I had. The important thing was that I found a cool company similar to Sphinx in which a suit and an 8am arrival time were not required.

I made sure to check the wording on each ad carefully before applying, looking for phrases like "young, hip company" or "fun start-up," clear indicators of a potential fit. But the only position I'd really set my heart on was for a fashion company in the city. They were looking for "energetic new employees" who would fit into their "easygoing work culture" (their wording, obviously). I was already sold. But even more exciting was that they wanted this person to not only assist with the online marketing of their products, but also with the photography. According to the job description, this person would photograph various products from their fashion line, edit the photos, upload the photos to their website, and then market these new products via social media outlets and mailing lists.

It was like someone had taken my marketing experience and

my photography passion and blended them into one hybrid dream job designed specifically for me.

Unfortunately, I had applied four days ago, but had yet to hear back. Hell, I hadn't even heard back from any of the jobs that I didn't want.

It's only been four days, I told myself. These things take time.

Patience was not my strong suit.

Just as I was about to start browsing career websites yet again, my cell phone rang. I looked down and saw my friend Jasmine's number on the display. I hesitated for a minute, debating on whether or not to pick up.

Jasmine was my former coworker at Sphinx. She worked in sales, thus the reason she and I became friends, since we were basically the only females in the sales and marketing departments. She first introduced herself to me at Sphinx's monthly First Friday party, and my initial impression was that she was the most beautiful black woman I'd ever seen. She had dark flawless skin, giant almond-shaped eyes, and perfect high cheekbones. She mainly wore suits and heels, as most sales people do, and even though she normally kept her hair pulled back, she always looked stunning.

Jasmine and I immediately became friends and she loved inviting me to her business happy hours because she could expense it on the company's dime. Two girls + free drinks = win-win. Ironically, we were friends for a good six months or so before I found out she was thirty-six. She didn't look a day over twenty-five.

Jasmine was one of the people I missed the most when I left LA. I had purposely limited my contact with her after leaving, because I didn't want to be reminded of anything that had to do with that time in my life. Jasmine loved to gossip. I knew she'd want to talk about Vincent, and I knew she'd ask about David. If I was going to move forward with my life, the last thing I wanted was to start digging up the very memories I'd been trying to bury.

As I held the phone in my hand, I remembered Renee scolding me for not opening up about my feelings. Would it really make me feel better? If I admitted aloud how lost and hopeless I felt? I really didn't want to dump my problems on anyone else, but as I looked down at the phone in my hand, I knew that if there was one person in the world who would never judge me, it was Jasmine.

"Hey Jas," I said.

"I've left you two messages." She was trying to sound mad. I could tell by the sound of her voice. But I knew her too well. I pictured her holding her cell, lips pursed, trying her hardest to keep a straight face.

"I know. I'm sorry. I've just… been keeping to myself lately."

"You're lucky I didn't fly out to Boston to find you. You know how salespeople are. Nothing stops us."

I couldn't help but laugh.

"Seriously, though, are you okay?" she asked.

"I'm fine. Just adjusting, that's all."

"Okay, well we don't have to talk about *him*." She pronounced the reference to David as though he was diseased. "But I do have two things I wanted to share with you."

During every phone conversation, Jasmine always listed the number of subjects to cover. I assumed this was because she talked so much it was easy to get sidetracked.

"But before I get into it, let me ask you a question," she continued. "When you say you're *adjusting*, what does that mean? Do you have a new job? New apartment? New boyfriend?"

"Not exactly. But I'm shopping around."

"For?"

I considered. "All three, actually."

"So, technically, you have nothing keeping you there."

"What are you getting at?"

"Well, we had a meeting today about a new event-management position that's opening up, and Jeff brought up your name."

Wow. Jeff Landry was Sphinx's CEO, and although I had spoken to him many times, I would never picture him nominating me for a job. I was surprised he even remembered who I was.

"Seriously?" I asked. "Why me?"

"I don't know. He just said that he thought you'd be great for it, and he asked if any of us had talked to you." She cleared her throat. "Which I *hadn't*, because…"

"I know. I've been avoiding everyone. I'm a terrible friend."

"Oh, no you're not," she said, sounding genuinely sad. "You're just going through a hard time. Trust me, we've all been there."

This was exactly why Jasmine was a good salesperson. She made you feel bad about something, then when you felt bad, she pretended she didn't mean to make you feel bad. I imagined this worked the same way with sales. She made you want to buy something, and then when you decided to buy it, she pretended she had nothing to do with it and it was all your idea.

Truthfully, the reason I didn't want to unleash my problems on her was because, after Renee left LA, Jasmine was the only close friend I had. When David got sick of hearing about how I missed Renee, I leaned on Jasmine. When David and I were on the outs, I went to Jasmine.

In short, Jasmine had already endured a lifetime of crisis-solving, and if I added any more problems to her plate, I should start paying her by the hour.

I will say, throughout everything, Jasmine never once complained or seemed irritated. She was a truly good listener. In most conversations, the other person pretends to listen, but really, they're already thinking of a response to revert the conversation back to them. Not Jasmine. She listened with genuine interest, never interrupted, and always offered great advice.

Advice that, of course, I never took. Because, let's be honest, no one asking for advice is ever really looking for advice. They're just looking for an excuse to talk about themselves and their problems. In the end, everyone ends up doing whatever they want anyway.

But I digress.

"Jas, I appreciate the heads-up," I said. "But after everything that happened with Vincent, there's no way I could ever work at

Sphinx again."

"Which is why I said I had *two* things to tell you."

Oooh. I could always gauge the gossip level by the tone of Jasmine's voice. The lower the voice, the juicier the dirt.

"Vincent was fired," she whispered into the phone.

"What?" I was almost positive I'd heard her incorrectly. "He was *fired*?"

"Yup."

"You're kidding." Vincent had worked at Sphinx forever. Probably close to a decade.

"It gets better." She paused, no doubt for effect. I was on the edge of my seat. "He was fired because he got caught sleeping with the receptionist."

"*Cheryl?*" I shrieked.

"Oh, God no!" Jasmine burst out laughing. "Cheryl's on medical leave, so they hired a temp to fill in. Her name's Sarah. Young blonde girl."

"Sounds about right."

"Yeah, I don't know all the details, but apparently the affair went sour, and by the end, everyone in the office knew."

"Ha!" The thought of Vincent's terminated ass being escorted out of the building was a visual in itself.

"Oh, it gets better."

God, I missed Jasmine.

"So, after word got out," she continued. "Another girl from the legal department admitted that he tried sleeping with her when she started working here, too. I think that's when they decided to fire him."

"Good thing I wasn't there," I said. "We could've gone all Tiger Woods on his ass."

"Well…" Jasmine's voice had now turned from gossipy to guilty. "I hope you're not mad, but after this happened, I told a few people that he was one of the reasons you left."

"You didn't."

"I did. But now people understand why you quit, you know? I mean, you liked working here…"

"I loved working there. But Jas, I'm here now. I can't go running back to LA every time a good opportunity arises."

"And you can't go running home every time a bad one arises, either."

Ouch. She had a point.

"Let me think about it," I said. "Give me some time to explore the job market here. Then… we can talk."

"That's fair," she agreed. "In the meantime, I'll put in a good word."

After I hung up the phone, I reverted to my original position at the kitchen table. I sat down and looked at the career site that was open on the laptop in front of me.

Well, that was fast. I'd heard once that if you asked the universe for something, it delivered. I just didn't think it had a four-day turnaround time.

Los Angeles, CA
April 2009

We spent the entire week together. Every day, every non-working hour, David and I were together. And when we weren't together, I was thinking about us being together.

I had never felt this way about anyone in my life. Ever. I couldn't get him out of my head. My apartment suddenly felt too big without him, like it was missing something. I didn't know what to do with myself. I just sat around in a daze, counting down the minutes until I could see him again. Waiting to feel complete. Whole.

I knew it was wrong, but it didn't feel wrong. We hadn't crossed any physical lines. We were just two people hanging out, watching movies, eating food, enjoying each other's company. David was fun. He made me laugh. He made me happy.

Of course, there was the small fact that I was beginning to fall head over heels for the guy, and for that, I probably should have stayed the hell away from him. But I couldn't. Because if I was being completely honest with myself, I couldn't remember anyone ever making me feel the way he did.

By the time Friday rolled around, I started to get nervous. Renee was flying home on Sunday, which meant I had exactly two days to come up with a plan. I wasn't sure whether I should be honest with her about spending the week with David, or if I should refrain from telling her, since she was going to break up with him anyway. But what if she didn't? What if they stayed together? And what did I expect to happen if they did break up?

My head was spinning. If they stayed together, there was no way I could be around them. And if they broke up, there was no way that David and I could be together. Either way, it was a lose-lose.

Ultimately, there was only one option. Honesty.

I picked up my cell and dialed Renee's number. She had called me the night before, but I had been out with David and still had no idea what I was going to tell her. My heart started to pound.

"Hey," she answered.

"Hey. How are you holding up?"

"I'm okay," she said. "I spent most the week helping my mom with funeral plans before the actual funeral. It hasn't been the most exciting visit." She sighed. "How are things with you? Did you have a good date with that Vincent guy?"

"Not exactly," I said. "Turns out he was married."

"You're kidding."

"I wish." I took this as my entrance cue. "But actually, David stopped over later that night to get some things, so he tried to cheer me up."

"Aw, that was nice of him."

"Yeah, it was." I paused, trying to force my voice to sound casual. "He said you've seemed distant lately. I think he knows you're going to break up with him."

"Huh?" She sounded distracted. "Oh, yeah. I was actually talking

to my mom about that last night. She thinks I'm being too picky."

That wasn't surprising. In a town the size of Rockland, there weren't many dating options. If you weren't married by the age of 25 to your high-school sweetheart, something was wrong with you. So I could understand why Mrs. Evans was confused as to why her daughter would throw away a handsome single bachelor without thinking twice. She was afraid Renee would never find anyone else.

"And what do you think?" I asked.

"Honestly, I haven't even had time to think about it. I didn't realize how much work goes into a funeral. We had to meet with the funeral directors, go over the obituary statements, pick out a casket..."

"Seriously?"

"Yeah," she said in a sad voice. "It was awful. I went with my mom and my uncle. The funeral director showed us all the caskets, and he's listing off these different prices and materials, and I could tell my mom and uncle were hardly even paying attention. Finally, my uncle said, 'To be honest, I don't like any of them.' Then he left the room." She lowered her voice to a whisper. "He's trying to keep it together, but I think he's taking it the hardest."

My heart sank. I had known Renee's Uncle John since we were kids. I didn't want to think about him burying his father.

My heart was also sunk because I had spent the entire week with my best friend's boyfriend, while she was back home picking out caskets for her dead grandfather.

I was a terrible person.

"My uncle and aunt are coming over tonight," she continued. "We're having dinner at my parents' house..."

I heard a muffled voice in the background, then Renee came back on the phone. "Sorry, my mom needs me downstairs." She lowered her voice again. "I can't wait to come home."

"Me too," I lied. "I'll see you Sunday."

As I hung up the phone, I felt a wave of disappointment. My attempted honesty had failed, my conscience was as guilty as it could get, and I still had no idea how Renee really felt about David.

74

And more importantly, what the hell was I going to tell her when she got home?

Chapter 11

Day twelve of the job-hunt. A week had passed and I hadn't received one response to my résumé. I was starting to get desperate. At this point, I was willing to take anything just to have an excuse to get out of the house.

I was officially starting to go insane. I had been snowed-in for days, was bored of the internet, and was beginning to have full-on conversations with myself.

Despite the number of positions I had applied to, I kept coming back to the fashion job. I'd re-read the description a million times, envisioning myself as a trendy photographer slash marketing guru at an über-sheik fashion company in the city. In my fantasy, the office had giant glass windows, the walls were painted an assortment of bright colors, and everyone had eclectic wardrobes and accessories. I would ride the train to work, clutching an oversized latte, as I absorbed the vibrant rush of the city.

Every other applicant's fantasy, no doubt.

The sound of my cell phone ringing put an unexpected halt to my daydream. My heart leaped when I noticed it was an unknown Boston number. Maybe it was them! The fashion company! Or any potential job that would give me a reason to leave my house!

"Hello?" I answered in my best friendly-yet-professional voice.

"Justine?" It was a man's voice. Deep. Sexy. Vaguely familiar.

"Yes?"

"It's Dylan."

"Oh." I couldn't even hide the disappointment.

"You're still waiting for that guy to call, aren't you?"

I had to laugh. Dylan was so direct. I'd never met anyone so blunt, yet so likeable at the same time. "Actually, I was hoping it was a job I'd applied for," I confessed. "How'd you get my number, anyway?"

"I took it from Renee's phone. I was hoping we could get together this week, if you're free. There's something I want to talk to you about."

"Um, okay," I said hesitantly. "Does Renee know?"

"No, and I want to keep it that way."

"No way," I said. "I'm not lying to her. You know what happened the last time I lied to her about something involving her boyfriend."

I heard Dylan chuckle on the other end. "Relax. I want to talk to you about planning a baby shower for her."

"Oh!" God, I really was a terrible friend. Renee was almost seven months pregnant and I hadn't given a second thought to her shower.

"I have some ideas I want to run by you," Dylan said. "Are you busy on Saturday?"

The thought was almost laughable. I wasn't busy ever. Even grocery shopping sounded fun right now. Anything to be around people.

"Saturday works for me," I said.

"Great. Meet me at Highland Kitchen at noon. We'll go over it then."

Before I could answer, he'd already hung up.

Los Angeles, CA
April 2009

On Friday night, David invited me to his apartment. I think he wanted to switch it up since we'd spent the majority of the week either at my place or out at bars. But for some reason, the thought of being at his house made me feel worse than I already did. Like I was trespassing on Renee and David's private space. David was used to hanging at my apartment, and bars were a common, social territory. But something about the two of us at his house didn't feel right.

I swallowed my guilt as I walked through his front door, expecting to find dozens of happy photos of David and Renee propped on the mantle. Luckily, David wasn't much of a decorator. His living room consisted of nothing but a beige sofa, a matching recliner, and a wooden coffee table. Then, of course, there was the gigantic flat-screen TV that took up the majority of the room. A typical bachelor pad.

By the time I got there, David was already sprawled out on the couch in a white t-shirt and gray sweatpants. He brown hair was matted to his head, like he'd just taken off his hat, and he was holding a shot glass in his right hand. I gave him a questioning look.

"You ever eat fireball candies as a kid?" he asked.

I nodded.

"Good." He pointed to a brown bottle on his coffee table. The label read "Fireball Cinnamon Whiskey."

"No way," I protested. To me, whiskey had always been a guy's drink.

He sat upright and poured a shot of brown liquid into another shot glass. "Trust me, it tastes exactly like those fireball candies. It doesn't taste anything like whiskey."

I took the glass reluctantly from his hand and sniffed it. It smelled exactly like cinnamon candy. I eyed the glass suspiciously for a minute, then downed the shot in one gulp.

"Oh, wow," I said, wiping my slightly watered eyes. Despite the spiciness, it was probably the most delicious shot I'd ever had. "That is good."

"Told you," he said, pouring us each another shot. We clinked our glasses together and downed the next one.

And the next.

And the next.

Finally, somewhere around midnight, the Fireball bottle was empty and David was sitting unusually close to me on the couch. It seemed as though the more we drank, the smaller the space between us became. He leaned over and passed me the final shot. Our knees were touching. My leg began to shake. I raised my glass to his in a final toast.

"To new friendships," I declared.

"Friendships," he repeated, smirking. Then he leaned over and whispered in my ear, "But what if I don't want to be just friends?"

I could smell his cinnamon breath, just inches from my face. His breath was warm in my ear. My heart began to race and I knew something was about to happen. Everything inside of me was gravitating toward him, like a magnet. I felt that tingly, happy drunk feeling buzzing all over my entire body, and all I wanted to do was lean over and kiss him.

David looked up at me, and even through hazy eyes I could still see the intensity behind them. He reached out and took my hand in his. I felt warm all over.

"Justine," he slurred. "I'm not just saying this because I've been drinking, but… I think I'm really falling for you."

I couldn't think of a reply. My head felt like it was in a cloud. I was floating somewhere high up above us. It was the one thing I needed to hear, but the last thing I wanted to hear. Because, despite the fact that I felt the exact same way, he was still my best friend's boyfriend.

Unfortunately, the logical part of my brain that was supposed to remind me of that was buried underneath vast quantities of whiskey.

I stared at him for a long time, but I couldn't make my mouth move. What could I say? That I loved the way his eyes widened when he looked at me? That I loved his mischievous little smile? That he made me feel as if love really did exist? That he was on my mind every waking minute we weren't together?

I couldn't. Because deep in my heart, there was someone I loved more than him. And even if she was 3,000 miles away, I could never do that to her.

David crinkled his brows together, searching my face for some sort of response. "I mean it," he said, resting his hand on my knee. "All I could think about this week was being with you. And when Renee comes home, that's not going to stop. Those feelings aren't going to go away." He lifted his gaze to mine. "I really think I'm falling in love with you."

I took a deep breath, trying to ignore the stinging sensation between my legs as his hand traveled up my knee to my thigh.

"But what about Renee?" I asked in a small voice.

"I've never felt this way about Renee," he said. "To be honest, I don't think I've ever felt this way about anyone."

Me neither, I thought to myself.

"And you said it yourself, she's going to break up with me anyway." He nudged me playfully.

"Well then, we'll have to wait." My voice was even smaller now. I was caving. We both knew it. I could feel myself pulling closer and closer to him, staring at his chest, his arms, picturing them around me. I wanted him so badly it hurt.

We stared in each other's eyes for a long time without speaking, until it felt like the heat between us had spiked the room temperature a hundred degrees. Finally, he threw me backwards on the couch and climbed on top of me.

"I don't want to wait," he said, burying his head in my neck. "I can't wait."

Oh God, I thought. This can't be happening.

Before I had time to process it, his mouth was on mine. He tasted like cinnamon and heat and everything I'd ever wanted. I wrapped his tongue around mine, sucked on his lips, released everything that had been bottled up inside me since the minute we'd met.

I can't do this, I thought. I should stop.

I have to stop.

It seemed like it was happening in slow motion. His hand up my *shirt. His lips on my neck, my chest. My shirt on the floor.*

This is so wrong.

This isn't happening.

His hands down my pants. His desire. Pressed against my leg. My body tingling everywhere.

God, I wanted him. Every part of me wanted him. It was like an unstoppable force had taken over. I knew it was wrong. I knew I had to stop.

I needed to stop.

But I couldn't stop.

And before I knew it, my legs were wrapped around him and I was being carried to the bedroom.

The bedroom of my best friend's boyfriend.

Guilt is always multiplied with a hangover. Alcohol not only impairs your judgment and your memory, it's also a depressor. So, in other words, any regrettable drunk action always feels one-hundred percent more regrettable the next day.

When I awoke in the morning, it took me a minute to realize where I was. White walls... navy bedspread... not much evidence otherwise. Then I looked over and saw David's sleeping face, buried in a navy-and-white-striped pillow.

It all came back to me in one giant wave. The whiskey. David telling me he loved me. His hands on me. Carrying me to the bedroom.

Oh God.

I was going to be sick.

I crept quietly out of bed, bolted to the bathroom, and threw up. I knew the whiskey was only partially to blame. The disgust I had for myself was far more nauseating.

How could I have done this? To Renee of all people? She was the last person in the world I'd ever want to hurt, and I'd committed the ultimate betrayal, all because I just wanted someone to love me.

Sadly, I did have someone who loved me. But apparently, she wasn't enough.

I thought back to all the times Renee had come to my defense. When my mom found a joint in my backpack and she took the rap for it. Letting me borrow money she didn't have for things I didn't need. Helping me with my UCLA application so we could move away together. She had always been the first person to come to my rescue.

I leaned over and threw up again.

Luckily, David's bathroom was stocked with Listerine, so I managed to pull myself together into a presentable human being again. I swished the minty liquid around in my mouth, swept my disheveled hair back into a ponytail, and stood up to face myself in the mirror.

To anyone else, I looked like an attractive, petite brunette with wide, blue eyes, a button nose, and a girl-next-door smile.

To me, I looked like a girl who was weak, selfish, and disgustingly disloyal. I had done the unthinkable, all because I couldn't control myself enough to stay loyal to my best friend.

I crept back into David's bed, trying my hardest not to wake him. Half of me wanted to slip my clothes on, sneak out the front door, and pretend this never happened, but I knew we had to talk.

David stirred beside me and his eyes fluttered open. I waited for his reaction to mirror mine, but all he did was smile and wrap his arms around me in a half-hug.

"Good morning, beautiful," he mumbled, cradling his head in my neck.

When I didn't respond, he looked up at me with sleepy eyes. Although he looked adorable in his half-conscious state, all my feelings for him had temporarily subsided. I just stared at him, unable to speak.

"Oh no," he said. "Don't look at me like that."

I lay back on the bed and rested my head on the pillow, turning to face him. "David, I… we…" I sighed. "We should never have…"

"Listen," he interjected, propping his head on his elbow. "I know what you're thinking, and I know how you're probably feeling right now. But I need you to know that I meant everything I said last night."

And there it was, my biggest fear, staring me right in the face. Instead of David agreeing that it was all a mistake and suggesting we never mention it again, it was even worse.

David was in love with me, too.

I didn't know what to say. No matter which direction I took, I couldn't win. I couldn't tell him I loved him, yet I couldn't pretend I didn't.

Unfortunately, I didn't have time to respond.

I heard her before I saw her. It happened so fast I didn't have time to react. The sound of footsteps in the hall. Doors closing and opening. Watching my best friend's expression change from excitement to confusion to shock. All in a matter of seconds.

And for as long as I live, I'll never be able to erase that image from my mind.

Chapter 12

Highland Kitchen was what Renee and I referred to as Somerville's "hipster hangout." It was located in the heart of Davis Square, and was well known for its Wednesday-night karaoke and homemade mac and cheese. The same crowd that frequented the local rock clubs also frequented Highland, so it was no wonder that Dylan chose it as our meeting spot.

I, of course, was early due to the excitement of having a reason to leave my house, so I took a seat in a corner booth and ordered a coffee while I waited for Dylan. As I sipped from my mug, I watched the converse-wearing, Pabst-drinking crew that flowed in and out, smiling to myself. It felt good to be back in the city. As much as I missed LA, there was something about Boston that just felt like home.

Dylan arrived at quarter past twelve wearing a black-leather jacket, black, ripped jeans, black combat boots and a black beanie cap. He was always dressed in black. A natural rock star, without even trying. He crossed the restaurant and sat down in the chair across from me.

"Hey," he greeted, grabbing one of the menus from the table. He removed his beanie cap, running his hands through his dark hair as he scanned the menu.

"Hi," I said, taking the other menu and flipping it open, even though I'd been studying it for the past twenty minutes and already knew what I wanted to order. I waited for Dylan to speak, but he seemed heavily engrossed in his brunch options. After a few minutes of silence, our waitress appeared to take our order.

"Coffee, pancakes, and bacon," Dylan said.

"Eggs Benedict," I said, stacking our menus on top of each other and handing them to her.

Once our waitress had disappeared, Dylan looked up at me for the first time since he'd arrived. It nearly made me jump. His eyes were a piercing shade of blue, but I never realized how piercing until seeing them in broad daylight. I'd only been around Dylan at night, usually at one of his shows, and even then, his gaze was intense. But now, his eyes practically glowed in the sunlight. It was like seeing a vampire during the day.

"Thanks for meeting me here," he said. "Renee's home a lot, so I figured it'd be easier to meet in person since I can't really talk when she's around."

I nodded.

"So, I was thinking of having the baby shower at my mom's house," he continued. "She loves Renee and offered to host it, and I thought it might be a good idea. Unless you had somewhere else in mind?"

I shook my head, embarrassed that I hadn't even given it a second thought. "No, I think that sounds great."

"Good." He seemed pleased that I'd agreed. "I know that typically only girls go to these things, but Renee isn't really into traditions, so I thought it might be fun to invite some of the guys. Maybe have a little music theme or something." He laughed and shook his head like he was embarrassed. "As you can probably tell, I don't have a clue about any of this."

It was at that moment that I knew exactly why Renee loved Dylan. He was everything he appeared not to be. In a good way. When I'd first met him, I had a hard time seeing what Renee found attractive in him. He had a small, emaciated frame, an oversized nose, and dressed like a homeless person. But after getting to know him, I understood. There was something about him that was just… sexy. He was an intoxicating conversationalist. He drew you in. And once you got past the brooding artist façade, he actually had a bigger heart than anyone.

"I think that's a good idea," I agreed. "I'll be honest, I don't know much about baby showers either, but you are supposed to have a theme. So I could get some music decorations…"

"Good, because I definitely don't want to be in charge of that," he said, smirking. "But I was thinking, if you want to invite the girls and handle the decorations, I'll invite the guys, and my mom can take care of the food. I'll tell Renee that we're having lunch at my mom's house so she doesn't suspect anything."

Our conversation was interrupted by the sound of his phone ringing. He looked down, then motioned for me to be quiet.

"Hey, babe," he said into the phone. "Yeah, I'm just grabbing some food with the guys, then we're heading to the studio." He paused. "Yeah, okay. Sounds good. I will."

"Renee?" I asked after he'd hung up the phone.

"Yeah. She wants me to…"

We were interrupted again, this time by the sound of my phone ringing. I looked down at the caller ID and felt a beat of panic rise in my stomach.

"Now she's calling me!" I yelled.

"So make something up," he replied calmly. "Or ignore it."

I scowled, staring down at my phone. I hated lying. Especially to her.

"Hey!" I said into the receiver, my voice a tad too cheery.

"Hey," she said. "What are you doing?"

"Oh I'm just…"

Shit. I hated making up lies on a whim. I should've thought this out ahead of time.

"I'm just going to…meet my mom," I stammered. "For lunch."

"Oh, tell her I said hi. Where are you guys going?"

"We're, um… I'm not sure yet."

God, I was terrible at this. Even Dylan was trying to control his laughter.

"I'm… meeting her at her house," I continued. "Then we're going to figure out where to go."

"Oh, okay. Dylan's at practice so I have the afternoon free. I wanted to see if you were around."

"I can come by afterward," I offered. "I'll call you when I'm done."

I hung up feeling a sense of déjà vu all over again. The last thing I wanted was to see my best friend face to face and be forced to pretend I wasn't just with her boyfriend. Although this time, it was entirely for her benefit.

I expected Dylan to reciprocate with a similar reaction, but as the waitress dropped off our two breakfast plates, the only thing he managed to say was," Thank God. I'm starving."

Los Angeles, CA
May 2009

It had been over a week and still no word from Renee. I kept replaying it over and over again in my head. The look in Renee's eyes when she recognized me. Her outline getting smaller as she disappeared out the front door. Trying to run after her. The sinking in my heart every time I came home to an empty apartment. Wondering if she'd ever walk through that door again.

The only thing that got me through the day was knowing that, eventually, she'd have to come home. As far as I could tell, she hadn't even stopped by to pack any overnight items. Her bedroom looked the exact same way it had looked since she'd left for Boston. So, at some point, she'd come back. And when she did, I would explain everything to her and beg her to forgive me.

At least this was what I thought, until I came home from Sphinx one night and found all her things gone.

It was like a knife in my heart. To anyone else, it wouldn't look like anything was missing. All our furniture was in its usual place, our pictures in their usual spots. But as my gaze caught the bookshelf, I noticed something out of the corner of my eye.

Half of the books were missing. Renee's half.

I then proceeded to her bedroom. Her bed and bureau were still there, but they were empty. No blankets or pillowcases on the bed, no pictures or stacks of makeup on the bureau. Slowly, I opened each drawer, one by one. Empty. All of them.

As a last-ditch effort, I ran to the closet, praying there would be something left, something she'd have to come back for. But again, nothing.

I walked back to the living room in a daze. Even though it was still full of our furniture and decorations, all I could see were the missing books on the shelf.

Sure, it wouldn't appear that anything was missing to an outsider. But to me, it might as well have been a vacant apartment. The Renee in our apartment was gone.

It couldn't have come at a more perfect time, really. Because of her family circumstances, Renee had turned in her final semester work early before she'd left for Boston. So there was nothing else keeping her here.

That's when it really hit me.

We'd been through so much together, from awkward teenage high-school years to California college graduation. And now, it was over.

She was gone.

And I had no one to blame but myself.

Picture the worst breakup you can imagine. The kind where you can't sleep, can't eat, break into random crying spurts, and walk around with a nervous stomachache that refuses to leave. The kind where you wake up in the morning and feel a momentary sensation of happiness, until reality sets in and you remember. And then the cycle continues all over again.

Now multiply that by ten.

That's how I felt without Renee.

I didn't go to work for the rest of the week. Instead, I told Vincent I'd come down with the flu, curled up on my couch, and watched every sad movie I owned. Only instead of seeing the characters on the screen, all I saw were two girls growing up together. Cutting photos of rock stars from magazines and hanging them on their walls. Passing notes in school hallways. Skipping class to hit the beach. Blasting Def Leppard while driving cross country. Cramming for finals with nachos and margaritas.

It was worse than any breakup I could imagine.

The way I saw it, breakups typically occurred with someone who was only a small part of your life. Sure, they were a big part of your life during that specific time period, but in the grand scheme of things, they were only a small percent of your overall life. Chances were, there would be several others with whom you'd have more or less the exact same relationship, and someday you'd look back and forget why you'd ever cried about any of them in the first place.

The problem was, Renee wasn't a small part of my life. She wasn't some guy I dated for a year who I'd probably forget about in six months. We'd grown up together and experienced everything together. She wasn't just a part of my life; she was a part of me.

And I had no idea where she was.

Was she staying with a friend in LA until she cooled down? Had she packed up her car and driven back to Boston? Now that school was over, she didn't have any reason to stay here, but I couldn't exactly call her parents to find out. That would be a tough one to explain.

So instead, I opted to mourn our friendship on my couch, in my pajamas, while stuffing my face with ice cream and avoiding David's calls.

He'd called at least a dozen times since that morning. I couldn't talk to him. Not now. Ironically, before this, he was all I could think about. Now, he was the last thing on my mind. And the last person I wanted to see.

Especially when he showed up at my door the following Saturday morning when I hadn't showered in three days. Going on four.

I knew the second I looked into his pleading eyes that this wasn't going to be easy. David was used to getting what he wanted, and he wouldn't give up without a fight. And right now, he wanted me.

"Please let me come in," he begged through the living-room door I'd half-opened.

"Not now, David." I wasn't ready to deal with this. I'd barely slept in weeks. Everything inside me was emotionally and physically exhausted.

"I'm coming in," he insisted, pushing the door open and stepping into the living room.

I lay down on the couch and closed my eyes. An easy surrender. I didn't have the energy to fight him. He sat down at the end of the couch and placed my legs on his lap.

"Please look at me," he asked.

I couldn't. Because I was afraid that the second I did, it would be over. All those feelings would come rushing back, and I'd eventually give in.

I couldn't. Not again. Not this time.

He grabbed my hands and held them in his. I felt his eyes on me.

"She left," I mumbled. "She's gone. All her things are gone. She's not coming back."

"I know," he said. "She sent an email to her manager saying that she wasn't coming back to work. Everyone thinks that after the funeral she decided to stay in Boston."

Of course. David and Renee worked together. I should have known she wouldn't go back there.

"So I'm guessing that's why you haven't been answering my calls," he continued.

I nodded.

I heard him sigh. I could picture him with his head down, contemplating what to say next.

"I'm sorry," he finally said. "I never meant for this to happen. I

know you guys have been friends for a long time."

I nodded again. There really wasn't much else to say.

"But," he continued. "That doesn't change how I feel about you, Justine. And after this week... I know you feel the same way."

What David didn't know was that I'd already had this conversation with him, in my head. Only in my fantasy, Renee had broken up with him, found the man of her dreams, and then granted me permission to date the man of mine.

Never in a million years had I pictured it this way.

At that moment, I finally opened my eyes. I looked him dead in the face, into his dark, desperate eyes, and all I could say was, "Please leave."

He stared at me in disbelief for a moment, looking like I'd slapped him. "You don't mean that."

I sat up and motioned to the door. "Go."

And as I watched him leave, for the first time I felt absolutely nothing.

Chapter 13

Nothing good has ever come after the sentence: "I need to talk to you about something."

Renee had dragged me to a clothing store in the Back Bay that was rumored to stock trendy baby attire. And by "trendy" she apparently meant "baby rock-star in training," because the entire store was lined with teeny tiny t-shirts with Zeppelin and AC/DC logos scrawled across the front. They even had baby beanie hats.

"Okay," I said cautiously as we crossed over to the shoe area. "What's up?"

Renee picked up a pair of pink baby Uggs, then looked at me with a concerned expression. "Do you think Dylan would cheat on me?"

"No," I said, without hesitation. It was a ridiculous question. Prior to meeting Dylan, it would've been a fair question, as musicians didn't have the greatest reputation when it came to monogamy. However, my preconceived stereotype was laid to rest the minute I met him. Dylan may have been a playboy in his previous life, but when it came to Renee, he was one-hundred percent faithful. I'd watched him at shows when he thought no one was looking, and he didn't have an inkling of a wandering eye.

Renee put the boots back on the shelf. "Last weekend, he told me he was going to band practice with the guys. But I talked to

Christian's girlfriend a few days ago, and she mentioned that they were at a wedding on Saturday."

Dammit. This was exactly what I had been afraid of. I took a deep breath and hoped my expression wouldn't give me away. "Well, did you ask him about it?"

"Yeah. He said they practiced without him."

"So, what's the problem?"

"Band practice without the drummer?" She looked at me skeptically. "I highly doubt it. Dylan always emphasizes that the band needs 'rhythm' when they rehearse."

"Renee, Dylan's a good guy. He'd never cheat on you."

"I know. I just have this funny feeling that he's hiding something. I can't shake it."

"I'm sure it's nothing," I said, trying my hardest to feign sincerity.

"Yeah, maybe you're right." She forced a smile.

I felt awful. The last thing I wanted was to lie to her, especially after she'd been gracious enough to give our friendship a second chance. But then I thought about the surprised look on her face when she walked into a living room full of friends and family and baby rock-star decorations, and I knew it was the right thing to do.

We walked back to the clothing section, where she immediately grabbed a Rolling Stones onesie and held it up for my approval.

I laughed, holding up a pink toddler tee with a giant skull on it. "How about this?"

"Too goth," she said, clearly missing my sarcasm. "And besides, I think I'm having a boy." She turned her attention back to the onesie. "I'm totally getting this."

"What if it's a girl?"

She shrugged. "The Rolling Stones are unisex."

After grabbing a pair of baby sunglasses, a t-shirt with a picture of a cassette tape on it, and another onesie that said "I'm with the Band" (all of which she insisted were unisex), we were officially at the checkout line.

"So, what's going on with you?" Renee asked, as we stood in

line behind a couple, who were chatting with the cashier. "Have you landed any interviews yet?"

"No," I said, defeated at the thought. "I need to find something soon, though. My parents usually start renting out the house by June."

"Have you asked them how long you can stay?"

I shook my head. "I've been avoiding them for weeks. I'm scared they're going to want me out before I find a job."

As soon as I said it, I felt my heart stop. We both realized it at the same time. I watched Renee's eyes narrow the minute I finished my sentence.

"I thought you had lunch with your mom last week," she said slowly. I could tell she was trying to sound normal, but there was an underlying accusatory tone in her voice.

Shit. Shit shit shit shit.

"I did," I said quickly. "But we didn't talk about the house. And other than that, I haven't really talked to them much."

She nodded as she moved toward the cashier, as if she was pretending to believe me.

But I could tell by the look on her face she didn't believe it for a second.

Los Angeles, CA
May 2009

I returned to work the following Monday. You'd think I had risen from the dead by the way Vincent was acting. He seemed to have long forgotten about our night at the Penthouse. Instead, it seemed like his infatuation for me had become ten times stronger. He brought me surprise lunches, found every excuse in the world to stop by my desk, and watched me with the same flirtatious expression I'd once adored. He even called me into his office to check on me, saying I'd seemed a little down lately.

Yeah. That was one way of putting it.

I could only assume this new attitude was due to the fact that, at the moment, I was very vulnerable. Not vulnerable enough to sleep with a married man, but pretty damn close. At this point, I was grateful to anyone who was nice to me, simply because I felt like if they knew the person I really was, they wouldn't be. And Vincent wasn't stupid. I was certain he'd had several successful seductions by preying on young women who felt very much like I did at the moment.

Fortunately, Vincent's new attitude was laid to rest the minute a bouquet of red roses was delivered to me that Thursday. From David, of course.

The whole situation was absurd. I had spent years searching for one guy who would love me, and now I had two.

They were just the wrong guys.

Even the disappointed look in Vincent's eyes once he noticed the flowers couldn't invoke any satisfaction in me at this point. I was numb. And it wasn't just Renee's absence that was really wearing on me, it was more the loathing I had for myself. I had caused a situation that could've been easily avoided had I possessed an ounce of self-love and self-discipline. And no matter how many times I went over it, I couldn't understand.

How could I say no to a married man, but give in to Renee's boyfriend? How could I be loyal to a complete stranger over my best friend?

After a week of repeated, non-stop questions, I found my answer.

Friday afternoon, just as I was gearing up for another depressing weekend alone, I crossed through the Sphinx lobby and found David waiting for me. He was sprawled out on a large leather chair, shoulders slumped, looking completely lost. Cheryl shot me a look that said, "He's not leaving until you go with him." And because I knew that was the truth, I agreed to have dinner with him at the Main Street Grill, the same restaurant where we'd dined previously. Only this time, it seemed far less appealing.

Main Street was a popular happy-hour spot, as it was conveniently located near all the high-rise business buildings in the Playa Del Rey area. It had a backyard barbecue kind of theme with picnic-style tables, in-house brewed beers, and appetizer selections that mainly consisted of oversized pretzels, wings, and cheese fries.

Despite the TGIF bliss surrounding me, I felt like I'd had the life sucked out of me. Much like I'd felt all week. It was hard to concentrate on David's words. I could see him trying, I could feel him trying, but I was dead inside.

He reiterated his feelings for me, over and over again. He sympathized with me. He asked me fair questions. What if Renee never spoke to me again? Could I be with him then? Or would I think of her every time I looked at him?

They were all reasonable questions, but I couldn't answer any of them. Because all I could think about was the thought of Renee never speaking to me again. A thought I couldn't fathom.

David's eyes became more and more desperate with each unanswered question, searching for something inside of me, anything to validate that what we'd had was real. But all I could do was pick apart the pretzel on my plate and tell him I didn't know. It wasn't the answer he was looking for, but it was the only answer I could give.

Because truthfully, I didn't know.

I didn't know if Renee and I would ever be friends again. And I didn't know if I'd ever be able to look at him without seeing her.

After David and I left the restaurant, he walked me through the parking lot in silence. He stopped when we reached my car, watching me with those crazy brown eyes that had once haunted me. Then he folded his arms around me and held me.

It was the longest, most intimate, hug I'd ever experienced. I held him tight, feeling the love between us, the emotions. I didn't want to let go.

When we finally pulled away from each other, he brought my left hand to his lips and kissed it gently, looking at me in a way that made my heart ache. A sad, desperate, longing look. A goodbye look.

"I won't bother you anymore," he said. "But please think about what I said."

I nodded, hopped into my car, and waited for him to pull away before bursting into tears.

I cried the entire way home. Conveniently, the next song on my iPod playlist was "Love Bites" by Def Leppard. I cranked up the volume to one of the sappiest songs of the eighties and cried. I cried all the way through Playa Del Rey, through Marina Del Rey, through Venice, through Santa Monica, until I arrived at my apartment in West LA.

And as soon as I walked through the door, it hit me.

I had been torturing myself, wondering how I could have betrayed Renee, and why I couldn't have just said no to David.

The answer was so fucking simple.

I was in love with him.

I was hopelessly, desperately, painfully in love with someone I couldn't stay away from.

Why else would I voluntarily hurt my best friend? Sure, I knew the golden rule: never go near any man your best friend has been involved with. But I had always believed that we don't choose love, love chooses us. We can't control who we fall in love with. I couldn't just flip a switch and stop the pain throbbing in my heart.

I didn't know what was worse, betraying my best friend or walking away from something that felt so real, and wondering if I'd ever feel that way about anyone again.

I lay down on my couch and sobbed. The memories that David and I had created in such a short amount of time flooded my mind. I had never opened myself up so completely to anyone. But there was something about him that was so contented, familiar even, like I could be myself with him. And he loved me. All of me.

At that moment, there was a knock at the door. My heart leaped. I raced to the door with tears streaming down my face, knowing exactly who was waiting on the other side.

Before I could even open it completely, his arms were around me, his lips brushing light kisses against my forehead.

"I love you," I said, burying my face in his chest to hide my tears.

"I love you. I love you. I love you."

"I know," he said, running his fingers through my hair. "I know."

And from that moment on, I was his. Completely. There was nothing I could do to fight it anymore. He had full control over me.

It was exhilarating. It was confusing.

And it was downright terrifying.

Chapter 14

I decided to take up meditation. Not because I had a spiritual breakthrough or anything, I was just running out of options and thought the local bookstore might be a good place for some insight.

After perusing the bookshelves for something that would help me piece my life back together, I came across a book called *My Kick-Ass Life*, which focused on how to use your positive energy in order to attract good things into your life. My first thought was that it sounded like a bunch of bologna, but considering the hole I'd dug for myself, I figured I had nothing to lose. I had to start somewhere.

I spent the rest of the afternoon curled up on my couch (or rather, my parents' couch, but according to the book, negative thoughts were the ultimate no-no), with my new life guide. The first chapter explained how our thoughts created our reality, and by mentally focusing on the things we wanted, we could ultimately attract these things into our lives. On the flipside, it also explained how negative thoughts and feelings could prevent us from gaining the things we want, and instead, those thoughts would attract more negative things into our lives, because that's what we're focusing on.

Well, then. Clearly, I had a lot to learn.

Instead of diving right into chapter two, I took a breather, grabbed a notebook and a pen, and began compiling a list of all the positive things I wanted to attract into my life. Because, in order to attract these things, I first had to figure out what they were.

What I want:
Love

I frowned and crossed that one off. I wasn't ready for that shit yet.

What I want (right now):
A job
An apartment (which will happen after achieving number one)

That seemed like a good start.

I then lay back on the couch, closed my eyes, and pictured myself landing the position of my dreams. Which, at the moment, was the fashion job I'd been obsessing over. According to the book, I had to believe that I could achieve the goal in order to make it happen.

I can land this job. I deserve this job. I love fashion. I am experienced in marketing. I am passionate about photography. I am perfect for this job.

My positive manifestations were interrupted by the sound of my cell ringing. I grabbed it from the coffee table and noticed an unfamiliar number on the display. I looked up at the ceiling and vowed that, if this was the fashion company calling me for an interview, I would meditate all day, every day, for the rest of my life.

"Hello?" I answered.

"Hello, may I speak with Justine please?" a male voice asked.

"This is Justine," I said eagerly, sitting upright.

"Hey, Justine. It's Walter Keller."

I can honestly say this was the first time I was ever disappointed by a phone call from a man who looked like Walter Keller.

"Hi Walter," I said, trying to hide my disappointment and failing miserably.

"Uh oh. Sounds like you're still waiting for a certain someone to call."

"Why does everyone say that?" I threw myself backward on the couch. "I was actually hoping you were one of the companies I sent my résumé to."

"Whatever you say." I could picture him smiling on the other end. The little-boy smile. "Well, the reason I'm calling is because I have a few people who are interested in the apartment you liked, but since you're a friend of Renee's, I wanted to check in with you first."

Oh, if only. If only I had my dream fashion-marketing-photography job... If only I had my spacious-modern-glass-shower apartment...

Sigh. Apparently chapter two was going on tonight's reading list too.

Los Angeles, CA
July 2009

Two months after Renee left, David and I moved in together. I know, I know. It was a stupid decision. But when it comes to love, there are no stupid decisions. Only impulsive ones that seem to make sense at the time. Which later turn out to be those "life lessons" you always hear about, AKA the things you would never, ever make the mistake of doing again.

Basically, it boiled down to four deciding factors:

1. I couldn't afford the rent alone.

2. The thought of living with a stranger was petrifying.

3. Renee hadn't returned any of my phone calls in the past two months, thus I took this as a final termination of our friendship.

4. I was so pathetically in love with David that I would've agreed to anything that increased our time together.

Sadly, over the past two months, we had become one of "those" couples. You know the type. The "no, you hang up first" couples. The "no, I love you more" couples. The couples that, when forced apart, spend every second whispering into their cell phones or giggling at their text messages or anxiously typing away on their instant messenger with a perma-grin glued to their faces.

So, naturally, when David came up with the brilliant plan that I should move in with him, I agreed.

At first, it was bliss. Granted, I missed Renee like crazy and still felt terrible about what I'd done, but David had me so brainwashed that we were these crazy cosmic soul mates that after a while, it was like he had replaced Renee. He had become my other half. My whole life. My everything.

"What if you had said no?" he'd always ask, every time I mentioned Renee. "What if you'd walked away from me? You'd still be thinking about me. Every time you were out with some guy, you'd be wishing he was me. And wondering if you'd ever meet someone you feel that way about. Is that what you want?"

I knew it wasn't. And I knew he was right. It was exactly why I'd done what I did. I was scared to death of living the rest of my life wondering if David was the one that got away, and resenting Renee for it, who didn't even want him in the first place.

And the more he said it, the more I believed it.

Everything started out perfectly. We redecorated his apartment and camped out like newlyweds, cooking dinner every weeknight, curling up with Rocky Road popcorn and movies on Friday nights, having breakfast in bed on Sundays. And when we weren't together, we were texting, calling, and emailing each other, counting down the hours until we'd be together again.

It was unhealthy. It was nerve-wracking. It was downright insane.

And yet, I'd never felt so alive in my life.

What I didn't realize was that when two people dive into a relationship head-first, eventually, someone has to come up for air.

Los Angeles, CA
May 2010

It had been almost a year since David and I moved in together when things slowly began to shift. I didn't even see it coming. Everything just unraveled and spiraled downhill so fast that before I knew it, it was like I was plummeting downstream without knowing how I got there in the first place.

Human emotions are funny that way. We're like magnets, and the more one person pulls away, the more the other clings to them. Which is a tactful way of describing the demise of my relationship.

It all started on a Sunday. The universal couple day. Saturdays were typically spent running errands, but Sundays were always our day. We'd spend the morning in bed, have breakfast, shower, and then watch David's sport of choice on the giant living-room flat-screen. Sometimes his friends would stop over and sometimes it was just the two of us. Then we'd order pizza and spend the rest of the night watching movies and maximizing our time together before the evil work week forced us apart yet again.

This particular Sunday was different. Instead of our typical morning sex/breakfast/sports routine, David informed me that he was going to meet his friends at an Irish bar on Wilshire to watch the game. With no extended invitation to yours truly.

It was at that moment, as soon as the door closed behind him, that I realized what deep shit I was in.

I had absolutely no idea what to do with myself.

What had happened to me? I used to be a person with friends! Hobbies! Goals! Now I felt like some sort of lost puppy, sadly eyeing the door until my master came back to give me attention.

In the span of a year, I had lost myself completely.

I tried to think of what I used to do in my spare time. Before David. Sure, Renee and I had spent a lot of that time together, but I still had my own life. I just couldn't seem to grasp sight of it anymore.

I tried to watch TV, but I found myself wishing that David was there to watch it with me. I went shopping, but found myself tempted to text David to see if he needed anything. I thought about how much I used to love photography, but now this trivial little hobby seemed *silly compared to my big, serious relationship.*

That was the beginning of the end. The more dependent I became on David, the more he pulled away. And the more he pulled away, the tighter I clung to him.

Pretty soon, sports Sunday with the guys became a weekly event. Our daily communications became less frequent. I could see it in his eyes when he looked at me – there was something missing. That crazed look of wanting was gone. I wasn't exciting to him anymore. He looked tired. Bored.

And instead of trying to make new friends, find new hobbies, do anything that involved not waiting around the house like a dog, I didn't. Instead, I watched his every move like the certified stalker I'd become, waiting for the axe to fall.

Which, naturally, it did.

David came home from work one night, sat down on the couch, and very calmly suggested that maybe I should move out.

I knew it was coming. I mean, who doesn't? No matter how much you try to convince yourself otherwise, you always know the truth.

But hearing it out loud made it real.

Of course, the first thing I thought of was Renee. This was why everyone said to never choose a guy over your friends. Who was I kidding? Did I actually think I could beat the odds?

And I had so many questions for him. What happened to us being meant for each other? What happened to the couple that couldn't make it through a whole day without each other? How could he throw that away?

"It's just… different now," he mumbled, running his hands through his smooth, brown hair. "You've changed." He looked at me like he was seeing me through different eyes. "When I first met you, you had such an… edge. You were funny and sarcastic and a little bit jaded from dating, but I loved that about you. And you were so excited about your job and your major and graduating and…" His voice trailed off. "It's just not the same."

"How?" My heart was pounding. I could feel tears rolling down

my cheeks and I couldn't stop them. Everything inside of me was pulling towards him, much like the first night we'd slept together, but this time it was different. I felt desperate. Out of control. I wanted to cling to him like a koala bear and beg him not to leave me. I wanted to convince him that I could change.

But even I knew how pitiful that sounded.

"It just seems like... that girl I fell in love with... she's gone. You agree to everything I say and everything I want and sometimes... I want you to fight back. Argue with me. Be passionate about something. You don't even talk about your job anymore. It's always what we're having for dinner, or what we're going to watch on TV. You don't ever go out with your friends."

"I don't have any friends," I said softly. "I lost the best friend I had. Because of you. Remember?"

"Renee isn't the only person in the world you can have as a friend. And speaking of Renee, she may have been critical and we may have had our differences, but she still stayed true to who she was when we were together."

Ouch. His words felt like they were ripping out my insides, one small part at a time.

"Well, maybe you should've stayed with her, then." I couldn't even attempt to sound vindictive. My voice was small, flat. Lifeless.

I expected him to argue with me, but instead he fell silent.

"Oh my God." I whispered, shaking my head in disbelief. "That's what you're thinking, isn't it?"

"I don't know." He covered his face with his hands. "Maybe we rushed into things. Maybe I should've tried to work it out with her. I don't know."

"I can't believe you!" I screamed. "I ruined a lifelong friendship because you insisted that we had this surreal connection, that we were meant for each other, and if I never gave it a chance, I'd regret it for the rest of my life. You chased me like I was the fucking goddamn Rolling Stones, and I really thought it was because you loved me, not because you're some asshole who gets off on chasing the impossible.

I'm not a fucking game, David. I'm a fucking person and I deserved to be treated like one."

God! That felt good.

I stood up from the couch, glaring down at him. He was looking at me like he'd never seen me before. I grabbed my purse from the loveseat and threw it over my shoulder.

"I'm going to stay at Jasmine's," I said, heading for the door. "I'll have my stuff out by tomorrow night."

Chapter 15

I always thought the pregnancy "glow" was something that people invented to make all the moms-to-be feel better about being fat and hormonal. Kind of like in the movie "Liar Liar" when Jim Carrey tells his son that "beauty on the inside" is just something that ugly people say.

However, I can honestly say that I'd never seen Renee look more gorgeous than she did at eight months pregnant.

Even way back when she lacked a fashion sense, Renee has always been beautiful. Aside from the fact that she's tall and blonde, she has incredible cheekbones and stunning, exotic-shaped green eyes. But there was something about her now that shone. Her skin and hair had never looked healthier, and aside from her stomach, the rest of her body looked exactly the same as before – a maternity bod most women would kill for.

But more importantly, she looked… happy.

The two of us had decided to spend our Friday night on her sofa since Dylan was playing a show. He'd finally moved their boxes into storage, so we had plenty of room to sprawl out for a girls' night. I had brought a collection of DVDs, a massive amount of Asian takeout, and a bottle of wine for myself, per Renee's request. She insisted that at least one of us should be able to enjoy a Friday-night buzz. No one loved to drink more than Renee.

"Mmm," she said, sniffing the top of the open wine bottle. "God, I miss this shit."

"One more month," I said, taking the bottle from her grasp. I reached over and moved two spider maki rolls onto my plate. Renee eyed them longingly. Apparently pregnant people weren't supposed to eat raw fish, so she'd been forced to order veggie rolls.

"That looks *so good*." She stared my roll down like it was Bradley Cooper.

"Renee, stop!" I yelled, giggling. I pushed the veggie plate toward her sulking face. "Well, speaking of good looks, your buddy Walter Keller called me last week."

"Oh?" Her eyed widened excitedly. "And?"

"He wanted to follow up about the apartment in Southie. I guess some people are interested in it."

Renee's eyes softened. "I'd love it if you moved to Southie. You'd be so close!"

"I know, but I still haven't heard back from any of the positions I've applied for."

"Well, it takes time. Just keep looking. You'll find something."

I took a sip of wine and looked around Renee's newly cleaned apartment, debating on whether or not to say what I was thinking. I knew I'd be in for a lecture if I disclosed too much, but it was impossible to keep anything from her.

"Jasmine called me about a job," I blurted out.

"Your friend in LA?"

I nodded. "I guess Sphinx's CEO nominated me for some event-management position that just opened up."

"That's great! Do they have an office in Boston?"

My eyes fell to the floor.

"Oh no. You are *not* thinking of going back to LA" She shook her head sternly, then paused. "Are you?"

"Not really. But if I don't find something by summer, I'm not sure what other options I'd have. There's no way in hell I'd ever move back in with my parents."

"And your unemployed ass can afford to move all the way back to LA?"

"Sphinx pays for relocation," I admitted. "Moving expenses and corporate housing for the first two months."

"So you have been considering it." She looked like she was going to kill me.

"No, it's just… a backup plan."

She rolled her eyes. "Justine, take it from me, you can't go running across the country every time your life goes sour."

"It worked out great for you!" I argued. "You met Dylan!"

"Yeah, but I also ran from my problems instead of dealing with them. Which means I spent over a year being upset with you and making assumptions instead of actually talking to you about how I felt and finding out how you felt."

"I know. But I think things worked out for the best. Otherwise, you wouldn't have met Dylan. And I wouldn't have been with David."

She looked at me curiously. "And that's bad because…"

I sighed. This was not my favorite subject. "Because if I hadn't got together with David, then I would've resented you for it. And I would've painted him as this perfect guy who got away and had him on a giant pedestal forever."

Part of me expected Renee to launch into a speech about how I always pick the wrong guys, or argue that what I did was wrong, but instead, she surprised me by breaking into a grin. "You know, I'm really proud of you."

My jaw dropped open. "Huh?"

"I'm proud of you," she repeated. "For opening up. I know you, Justine, and you hold everything in. You don't want to seem vulnerable so you keep all your feelings to yourself and you don't let anyone in, not even me. And yes, what you did with David was shitty, but when you explain it to me like you just did, it helps me understand. And even though I think it could've been handled differently, part of me knows you're right. I know how persuasive

David can be, and let's face it, I didn't want to be with him anyway. I think my ego was just hurt, and I was hurt that you felt like you couldn't talk to me about how you felt."

"It just happened so fast," I said in a soft voice. "And before I knew it… it was too late."

"I know. And you're probably right. You either would've resented me for not being able to be with him, or he would've pursued you until you finally gave in, at which point I would've resented you." She shrugged. "It happened the only way it could have."

"Well, I'm proud of you, too," I said, taking another sip from my glass. Between my wine buzz and Renee's hormones, we were seconds away from an estrogen-filled sob fest. "You're… incredible. Honestly, if you'd done the same thing to me, I don't know if I'd be half as forgiving as you."

"Yeah you would," she said matter-of-factly. "You don't give yourself as much credit as you deserve."

"I've been meditating," I spat out, hiding my face in my hands. That was the wine talking.

"*You?*" Renee asked, exasperated. I knew what she was thinking. I was the type of person who wouldn't be caught dead in the self-help section.

I nodded, embarrassed. "I bought a book about how to think positively in order to bring good things into your life. And to be honest, so far, it's pretty… awesome."

Renee looked like she was about to fall off her chair. "Damn. You really are desperate for a job, huh?"

Los Angeles, CA
June 2010

I moved in with Jasmine shortly after David and I broke up. Jasmine and I had become really close over the past year, ever since Sphinx turned my internship into a full-time position after graduation. Not to mention, after the downfall of Renee and now David, she was

110

really the only person I had left.

After Jasmine insisted that I stay with her, I went to David's place while he was at work, packed up all my things, and moved them into Jasmine's house.

And then, I proceeded to lose my mind.

The first few days were a blur. I couldn't even process what was happening. I just absentmindedly carried my boxes into Jasmine's house, dumped them onto the floor, and stared at them. Fortunately, Jasmine owned a decent-sized house in Culver City and lived alone, so there was plenty of room for my things. Unfortunately, I was the last person in the world that anyone would want as a roommate.

I managed to keep it together when Jasmine was home, but the second she left for work, I lost it. I tried to eat, sleep, watch TV, but all I could think of was David. I replayed our memories in my head. I analyzed every conversation, every experience, every detail. I cried until I didn't have any tears left.

Then came the denial.

After the initial shock wore off, I decided that maybe I had jumped the gun by moving out. I convinced myself that once David had some time to himself, he would see how much he missed me and realize he'd made a huge mistake. He just needed a little space. Then he'd remember the way our relationship used to be and want me back.

So naturally, I did what every insane ex-girlfriend does. I drunk-dialed him.

Jasmine had gone to meet one of her clients at a happy hour, leaving me all by my lonesome. Thus, I proceeded to drink an entire bottle of wine, which resulted in me leaving David a completely asinine voicemail that consisted of slurring, crying, and longwinded ramblings that I was convinced made complete sense at the time. Which then resulted in me psychotically watching my silent phone like a shoplifter for the next week.

Note to self: the recently dumped need a live-in babysitter.

It's funny how people's brains work when they get dumped. Instead of attempting to react somewhat rational, we do the complete opposite.

We put this person on the highest pedestal possible, and suddenly the dumper becomes this saintly creature that we'd do anything to see and touch again. They become Jesus. Brad Pitt. The perfect, unattainable human being. All of their bad qualities magically vanish, and we can only remember the good. Our brains conveniently erase all of the fights, all of the times he left the toilet seat up, and instead we remember that one time he bought us flowers, that first kiss, the way he smiled. Meanwhile, we should be hating the bastard for hacking our heart into tiny pieces.

After several tortuous days staring at my mean, mocking, silent phone, I devised one final plan that I was sure would make me feel better. I knew that David typically got home from work around 6.30, so brainiac me thought it would be a genius idea to stop by his place and talk to him face to face. I figured the best-case scenario was that once he saw me he would remember why he fell in love with me in the first place and want to work things out. And worst-case scenario, if he told me to take a flying leap out of his life permanently, at least I'd have some closure. A girl's gotta have her closure.

What I didn't expect was his pitch-dark, vacant apartment to send my mental state into a whole new whirlwind of crazy.

Where was he? Why wasn't he home? Was he out on a date? Could he have met someone already?

Alas, I probably should have given myself some time off before returning to work.

The following morning, Vincent called me into his office and asked me to shut the door. That was never a good sign. None of the managers at Sphinx ever shut their doors unless they were discussing confidential company info, gossiping, or reprimanding an employee.

I closed the door behind me and took a seat across from him, preparing for the worst.

"Justine, I know you're having some personal problems right now," he began, looking at me with concerned eyes. "And I just want you to know that if you need to take more time to sort things out, it's okay with me."

I waited for him to continue. "Is that it?" I asked. "That's why you wanted to see me?"

"Well, yes," he said hesitantly. "I don't want your work to suffer because you're not focused. And a few things were brought to my attention this morning that I need to address with you."

"Okay. What sort of things?"

He shifted in his seat, visibly uncomfortable. "Well, this is hard for me, because I like you as a person and I don't want to come down on you. But when you updated the company Facebook page this morning with our new Galactic game info, you forgot to include the link to the trailer. We have over 300,000 followers, so it's not exactly the best representation for the company."

"I'm sorry," I said flatly, even though I wasn't the slightest bit apologetic. Sphinx's reputation was the least of my concerns.

"And the weekly marketing report you sent out, you forgot to include me on the email." He waved his hand like he was sweeping the issue under the rug. "But again, I'm not trying to be hard on you. You're always efficient at your job, so I just want to make sure that you're okay."

I felt tears well up in the corners of my eyes. "No, I'm not okay," I blurted out, wiping my cheeks. "My boyfriend left me, my best friend won't speak to me, and I have no place to live." I grabbed a Kleenex from a box on his desk and wiped my nose. "I am definitely not okay."

Vincent inched closer to me. "Justine, these situations are never easy, but you'll get through it. Just please know that I will help you in any way I can. If you need any help financially to get settled into a new apartment, let me know. Seriously. Anything you need."

For a brief second, in my fragile state, I thought that maybe I had misjudged Vincent. At that moment, sitting across from me, he seemed like such a concerned, caring, father figure who genuinely looked out for people. Maybe he was just staying in an unhappy marriage because he loved his son. Maybe flirting with young women was the only way he felt any sort of love anymore. Maybe I had been too hard on him.

"Vincent, thank you for offering," I said. "But honestly, I could never take any money from you. I don't know when I'd even be able to pay you back."

Vincent slid even further forward in his seat, taking both of my hands in his. "Oh, I'm sure we could think of some other way for you to pay me back," he whispered, grinning devilishly.

Or maybe he was still the same cheating slimeball that got his kicks preying on young, vulnerable women.

At that moment, something in me exploded. Memories of Vincent at the Penthouse, Renee's empty room, David's bored eyes. They all came in one giant wave, like a fire slowly spreading throughout my entire body.

"You know what, Vincent," I said, rising from my chair. "I'm done."

He looked at me with a confused expression. "With?"

"This." I motioned around his office. To the walls of the kick-ass company I was about to leave. To the view of the beautiful city that was about to be behind me. To the life I had thought would make me happy. "All of this. I'm done."

As I walked through Sphinx's parking lot carrying a small box of my personal items, I was overcome with a sense of freedom. You would think that losing everything would leave me feeling empty and alone, but it was the exact opposite. I had officially hit rock bottom, which meant there was only one direction that my life could go.

Onward and upward, baby.

I was done crying. And moping. And feeling sorry for myself. Instead, I was going to take initiative and get my life back on track.

Which, unfortunately, had to start with a very uncomfortable phone call.

Beth Broadley was a childhood friend of Renee's and the one person who would undoubtedly know of her whereabouts, besides Renee's parents. And I sure as hell wasn't calling them.

Beth had become an acquaintance of mine through Renee, but she hadn't hung around with us a lot in high school. Beth was more of a relationship girl and always had steady boyfriends, whereas Renee and I were more of the party-girl type. I liked Beth, but she was sometimes a little too blunt for my taste, which was exactly why I was dreading the phone call I was about to make.

But shit, if I was going to get my life back on track, I had to start somewhere.

I drove down Lincoln Boulevard with my Bluetooth in my ear, nervously tapping the steering wheel until Beth answered. It took a good five seconds before she responded to my introduction.

"Hi," she said slowly, as if she was trying to decipher if it was really me or a prank caller. "How... um... what are..."

"I'm sure you know the whole story," I interrupted. "And I'm sure I'm the last person you want to talk to right now. But I need your help."

I expected some sort of rebuttal, or a lecture about what a terrible, heartless person I was, but to my surprise, all she said was, "Okay."

And then, everything poured out of me – from my date with Vincent to spending the week with David to quitting my job at Sphinx. Everything. And before I knew it, over an hour had passed and I was sitting in my car in Jasmine's driveway, crying to the one person I never thought would listen.

"Justine, I know you love Renee, and I know you would never intentionally hurt her," Beth sympathized. "And deep down, Renee knows that too. She was just too hurt to talk to you, and rightfully so. But the good thing about Renee is that she's a very forgiving person, and eventually, she's going to come around."

"I hope so," I said. "I miss her, Beth. I know I completely screwed up and she might never forgive me, but I have to try."

"Well, luckily, she met someone," Beth said. "And to be honest, they're perfect for each other. She's definitely over David, I just don't know if she's over feeling hurt by you. But I think it's worth an explanation."

"So what do you think I should do?"

"Well, are you planning on staying in LA?"

"Hmm… let me see. I have no job, no place to live…"

Beth burst out laughing. "Well there's your answer. If I were you, I'd get my ass on the first plane out and go get my best friend back."

Boston, MA
July 2010

I knew which apartment was Beth's before even looking at the door number. Her patio was lined with sunflowers, hanging beads, mismatched chairs, patchwork quilts, and a giant tie-dye tapestry in the center. Very boho chic. Very Beth.

My stomach was in knots as I ascended the stairs. As luck would have it, just as I was finally settled back in Boston and had my apology speech prepared and ready to go, Beth dropped the bomb that Renee and her new boyfriend, Dylan, had broken up. Or "had a falling- out," as Beth put it. Essentially the worst time I could ever attempt to make amends, but Beth seemed pretty confident that Renee and Dylan would work things out.

Beth's encouragement was the only reason I was standing at her front door, heart pounding, ready to face my estranged best friend who I hadn't seen in over a year. According to Beth, Renee was staying with her temporarily because she and Dylan had lived in the same building. Beth had called me earlier that day to let me know that she was going to her boyfriend's house after work, so Renee would be alone at the apartment.

Before I could lose my nerve, I took a deep breath and knocked on the door. I'm not sure how much time passed before Renee opened it, it could've been ten seconds or ten minutes, but it was the longest waiting period of my life.

And there she was. My beautiful best friend, standing in front of me, with a mixed expression of confusion and shock. She looked different somehow, but I couldn't pinpoint why. I studied her face, searching for an unspoken answer. Some indication of how the conversation was going to go.

As Renee stared at me in silence, I wondered if coming here was the right decision. After Beth told me about everything that happened with Dylan, I wasn't sure I could go through with it. But then I thought about how much I had hurt Renee, and how much she was hurting now. I couldn't give up without trying one last time.

"If you want me to leave, just say so," I said; the same line I had rehearsed a hundred times on the way over. "Beth told me what was going on and I just… I felt so awful. I really wanted to see you, and see how you were doing. But if my being here is completely inappropriate and you think I should go, I will."

I waited for her to slam the door in my face, to scream at me, to do… something. But instead she just stared. And stared. And said nothing.

I looked down at the ground, realizing I shouldn't have come. What was I thinking? That we'd forget the last year and act like nothing had happened? That we'd pick up where we left off? I had made my decision. I had chosen David. I couldn't take it back now. And I couldn't expect her to ever forgive me for it.

"It's okay," I said, my heart heavy with disappointment. "I completely understand."

I turned toward the stairs, trying to hold it together. It wasn't surprising, really. There was just a small part of me that hoped Beth was right, that Renee would forgive me once time had passed. That she'd realize I made a mistake, but our friendship was too valuable to throw away.

Wishful thinking.

I walked to the stairs, hoping she would say something, anything, even if it was that she never wanted to see me again. At least then I'd know. I wouldn't be left wondering.

I was at the first step when I heard the door open behind me.

"Wait," she said.

I spun around slowly, part of me afraid of what she was about to say and part of me relieved that there would be no more wondering. No more unanswered questions.

Before I could say anything, she reached out and threw her arms around me.

My heart heaved with relief as I fell into her, trying to find the right words. But before I could say anything, she pulled back to face me, smiled, and invited me in for dinner.

And just like that, my best friend was back.

Chapter 16

Dylan was a creature of habit. For our second baby-shower meeting, he had picked the same meeting spot, same day, same time, same meal, and wore more or less the same outfit. Highland Kitchen. Saturday. Noon. Coffee, pancakes, bacon. Black jacket, black shirt, black hat. The only difference was that this time his jeans were blue.

"Did your mom take care of the catering?" I asked, taking a bite of my chocolate-chip pancakes. After seeing Dylan's breakfast replica, I figured at least one of us should switch up our routine. Especially since *My Kick-Ass Life* placed a heavy emphasis on the belief that change was the key to success. It said that, even by changing little things, like going to a different supermarket or taking a new route to work, you were forcing yourself to step out of your comfort zone and face your fear of the unknown, thus inviting new and awesome things into your life.

And hell, if anything was going to jump-start my new-and-improved life, chocolate-chip pancakes were the way to go.

Dylan nodded, pulling a piece of notebook paper from his pocket. He was funny like that. Instead of emailing details or keeping notes stored in his cell phone like most people would, Dylan wrote everything down. Every time I'd been to a show, the back room was always filled with Dylan's strewn papers – directions to venues, addresses, song lyrics, chords. No wonder he needed Renee to help manage the band. A tech-illiterate leader was never good for business.

"Yeah, the food is all set," Dylan said, reading through the crumpled piece of paper. "My mom's ordering from this organic place since Renee's a bit of a health nut these days. Did you get all the decorations?"

The shower was set to take place next weekend at Dylan's mom's house. While most people hated planning showers, I was grateful for the temporary distraction from my uneventful life. And surprisingly, picking our music-themed decorations had turned out to be pretty fun.

"I did," I said, pulling out a bag of items I'd brought to show him. I passed him a necklace with a backstage pass attached that said "VIP Mom," a hanging pink-and-blue banner that spelled out "rock and roll" on little records, and a photo of guitar-shaped cookies I had ordered from a local bakery. "Aren't these cute?"

Dylan inspected each item I'd given him. "These are cute," he agreed, looking surprised by his sudden interest in shower decorations.

"Wait till you see the invitations," I said, removing one from my purse. I stood up and slid into the booth next to him, walking him through the entire layout. The shower invitations had the words "Rock the Cradle" scrawled across the top and a giant guitar in the center. At the bottom were Renee and Dylan's names, followed by the shower date and time and Dylan's mom's address.

Dylan scooted a little closer to me, reading the text over my shoulder. The layout was supposed to resemble a concert poster, where Renee and Dylan's names were the headlining act, and the date, time, and address were the venue details. I was amazed at how much rock-and-roll baby-shower material existed.

"This is great," Dylan said, shaking his head. "I can't believe you were able to find all this stuff." His glowing eyes met mine, startling me as usual. "Seriously, thanks so much for your help with this. Renee is going to love it."

"I know," I said. "We have to make sure she's surprised. I was thinking that maybe you should bring her to your mom's around 1.30, just in case anyone's late. I put 1 o'clock on the invites…"

My voice trailed off as my gaze fell upon the entrance to Highland Kitchen. A familiar feeling began to spread throughout my entire body as soon as I realized what was happening. A speedball of pain, regret, reminiscence.

No, I thought, my eyes growing wider. No. No. No.

This is not happening.

Not again.

My heart shifted into overdrive as I watched Renee stroll cautiously through the front door, looking around the restaurant like a lost child. Her sad, scared eyes floated from table to table until they fell on Dylan and me. Squeezed in next to each other in a corner booth. Knees together. Elbows touching. Mirrored guilty expressions.

I could only imagine what it looked like.

She approached the table like she was entering a war zone. The look on her face changed from disbelief to surprise to anger.

"I knew it," she said softly, shutting her eyes tight. When she opened them, it was like she was seeing us for the first time. She squinted at Dylan, like he had suddenly transformed into a complete stranger. "Band practice without Christian…" Her gaze shifted to me. "Lunch with your mom…" Her eyes fell to the ground. "I knew it."

My entire body began to shake, as this was exactly what I had been afraid of since the beginning. No matter how much I tried to convince myself that this was for Renee's benefit, I couldn't help but experience a resurrection of regret every time I met with Dylan.

Surprisingly, when I looked over at Dylan with fear in my eyes, he was unbelievably calm. Of course he was. He didn't have anything to feel bad about. I, on the other hand, was a different story. Renee may have forgiven me for what happened with David, but she'd never forget. No one ever forgets.

"Renee, relax," Dylan said in an even tone. "We were just planning a surprise for you."

God, he was so cool, so composed. For a second, I was able to convince myself that maybe I'd overreacted. Maybe it wasn't a big deal. Maybe we could just explain everything to her and she'd understand and everything would be fine…

"Oh, I'm surprised all right," she snapped, her voice starting to rise. "Let me see, I catch both of you lying to me, so I decide to follow Dylan to see for myself if I'm crazy, and what do you know? I find the two of you snuggled up together in the corner."

"Renee, sit down and hear us out for a second." Dylan motioned to the seat across from us.

"No, I'd like you to explain something first." She was seething, spitting out her words between clenched teeth. "If you two are so busy planning something for me, then why the *fuck* is she practically sitting on your *fucking* lap? Is that part of the surprise too? To sneak around and get cozy with my best friend when I'm not looking?" She shot me a look of disgust. "God knows, it wouldn't be the first time."

"Jesus Christ," Dylan mumbled, hanging his head in frustration. "Knock it off. You're starting to cause a scene."

"Seriously, it's not like that at all," I said. "We were just planning…"

"It's not like what, Justine?" she yelled. She wasn't even attempting to keep her cool anymore. "Like you fucking my boyfriend? Because we all know you'd never do that…"

"Enough!" Dylan yelled, slamming his hand down on the table.

"How could you do this?" Renee was screaming now, her arms flailing in the air. "What, once wasn't enough? You have to take him, too?"

I felt my cheeks flush crimson. Everyone in the restaurant was starting to stare. I couldn't believe that all this time, I'd thought things were back to normal with us. I was so grateful for my second chance, when in reality, I hadn't been given a second chance at all. All I'd been given was a grace period before I inevitably screwed up again.

I stood up and walked over to her, standing so close that our faces were almost touching. In a low voice, I said, "I have apologized to you a million times about David. You said that you understood, and that you forgave me, and that you trusted me. Clearly, I'm not the only one who's being dishonest here." I felt my jaw harden. "You may never be able to trust me, but when I told you that I'd never do that to you again, I meant it."

I leaned over, grabbed the bag of shower decorations from the table, and shoved them into her arms. "You know, I didn't expect you to forgive and forget. But I expected you to at least try."

I glanced back at Dylan before heading to the door. "Tell your mom I'm sorry about the shower."

I waited until I was safe inside my car before allowing myself to cry. This was due to several reasons, mainly because a) I didn't want to cause more of a scene than I already had at Highland Kitchen, and b) Renee was only part of the reason I was crying.

Sure, her words hurt like hell, but I also knew that she was pregnant and hormonal, and catching your best friend sneaking around with your boyfriend for the second time is bound to make a person say some crazy shit. But it was more than that.

The truth was, as hard as I'd tried to fight it, I just couldn't shake the feeling that I didn't belong here. Ever since I had moved back home, it was like I was trying to turn my life into something it once was, and failing miserably.

As much as I hated to admit it, the only time I could remember being truly happy was when I was in LA. I had a kick-ass job, a great apartment, and friends I didn't appreciate until it was too late.

Now, I had no job, no apartment, and a best friend who hated me.

The more I thought about it, the more I realized how important change really was. Instead of moving back to Boston and clinging to what was comfortable, I could have stayed in LA, held on to my great position, and made a wholehearted attempt to start over on my own. I could have tried to meet new people and grow my friendships, especially with Jasmine. She had been nothing but sweet and caring ever since I'd met her, yet I had never made any sort of an effort because, in my mind, I had Renee, and she was all I needed.

And look where that got me.

I wiped the tears from my eyes, took a deep breath, and picked up my cell phone. It rang three times before she answered.

"Hey, Jas," I said into the receiver. "So… tell me about this event-management job."

Chapter 17

It was as if LA had been expecting me. Literally. I couldn't have asked for a more inviting reunion. The second the plane touched down at LAX, the sunshine practically enveloped me in a welcoming hug.

Most non-Cal natives had a tendency to subscribe to the false notion that Southern California was similar to Southern Florida, where the weather was, for the most part, really hot. It wasn't. With the exception of summer, the temperature was generally in the sixties and seventies year-round, which was something that a Boston native could never complain about, especially when said native was flying there in the bone-chilling month of January.

However, every once in a while, LA had a fluke winter week where it was all sunshine, all eighty degrees, all day.

And don't you know, this just happened to be one of those weeks.

I could practically taste the happiness from my former existence as soon as I stepped into the crisp desert air. Palm trees. Hot breeze. Sun on my skin. Life. All around me. There was no life in Cape Cod in the winter. No people, no streetlights. Zilch. In LA, you were surrounded by life. People, energy, noise. Everywhere.

Even though it had only been six months, it felt like I had lived here in another life.

Jasmine's silver Mercedes was already parked curbside, waiting for me. She bolted from the car as soon as she saw me, barreling toward me in her fitted beige suit, her bright, white teeth gleaming. She wrapped her arms around me in a tight hug, then held me out at arm's length, staring me down like a mother who'd just been reunited with her child.

"How are you?" The enthusiasm in her voice indicated the question was less a formality and more a genuine concern for my wellbeing. "You look great."

"I look like hell." I glanced down at my yoga pants, sweatshirt, disheveled side ponytail.

"You look *great*." Her firm tone implied there would be no arguing. She reached down and emptied my suitcase into her trunk before I could object. "Now, let's go to my place and get you cleaned up. Because you, little lady, have an interview this afternoon." She shot me a knowing look. "And you know how much Michelle hates it when people are late."

God, it felt good to be home. Wherever that was anymore.

Michelle Lawrence had the body of a peanut and the presence of a tornado. She stood just above five feet tall, with a tiny, petite frame, black hair that fell a few inches past her shoulders, and a smile that could fool anyone into thinking she was just as sweet as she looked.

Until you got to know her.

At age 35, Michelle was the youngest Vice President at Sphinx. And from what I'd heard, she'd earned her title. The rumor was that during a trip to Sphinx's Tokyo office, Michelle was so disgusted with a new game trailer that the Tokyo management team had created that she reduced one of the executives to tears. Apparently, she tore him apart so badly that he had to leave the meeting and come back once he'd composed himself. The executive then wrote an email to the CEO singing Michelle praises, saying he'd never seen someone so passionate about gaming throughout his entire career.

Thus, Michelle Lawrence, the legend, was born.

Don't get me wrong, on a day-to-day basis, Michelle was generally all smiles and polite exchanges. She just wasn't someone I'd ever want to piss off.

Stepping into Sphinx's lobby was like a time warp. As I glanced around the room, my memory was instantly flooded with images of David sprawled out on the leather couch in his baseball cap waiting anxiously for me. The way my heart jumped at the sight of him. The electrical charge I felt being in his presence.

Change, I repeated silently to myself, resisting the urge to turn around and sprint to the elevator. There is no more David. No more Vincent. Only better people and bigger opportunities.

Cheryl was still out on medical leave and I assumed Vincent's latest victim had quit, based on the fact that I was greeted by a small Asian women when I entered the lobby. I gave her my name and took a seat until Michelle welcomed me a few minutes later.

"Hey there!" she said in her deep, smoker's voice, hugging me like we were old friends. I forgot how nice everyone was in California. Even the cut-throat VP had a soft side. I followed her into her office, waving to a few familiar faces along the way. No one looked surprised to see me. Sphinx was a relatively small office, so I assumed word had traveled fast.

I shut Michelle's office door behind us and sat down across from her. Her office looked exactly the same as it had six months prior – black-and-red leather couch stuffed in the corner, gaming posters on the walls, party photos on her desk. In addition to her tough work reputation, Michelle was also notorious for her chain-smoking habit and excessive tequila-shot intake. Apparently she could drink all the guys in the office under the table.

After a few minutes of small talk, Michelle got down to business. "So, I heard that one of the reasons you resigned was because of Vincent," she said, her face stone-cold. "And if so, that's completely understandable. We don't have to get into it. All I'll say is that I'm glad he's gone." She flashed me a genuine smile. "And I'm glad you're here now."

"Me too."

"Good." She picked up a piece of paper with a job description printed on it. "Because I think you'd be perfect for this position."

Wow. It wasn't every day that you received a compliment from Michelle Lawrence. "Thank you," I stammered. "Um… may I ask why?"

"Well, this person is going to be organizing all of our events," she said, reading through the bulleted lines. "E3, Comic-Con, Pax… all of them. And since you were in our marketing department for a year, you're already familiar with these events and the preparation that goes into them. Not to mention this person needs to be extremely organized, which I already know that you are, based on your previous work here."

"Thank you," I repeated, still stunned at the flow of praises.

"In addition to the business aspects of things, this person also needs to have an outgoing personality," she continued. "A good portion of the job is interacting with people, mainly the event organizers and attendees. So with your knowledge of the business and your personality, you'd be a great person to represent the company." Her lips curled upward. "And let's face it, your looks don't hurt either."

I burst out laughing. "So, I'm gonna be a booth babe?"

"Hey, sex sells," she joked. "But in all seriousness, if you want the job, it's yours. I've already talked to the team here and everyone agrees that you'd be the best person for it. We'd take care of your relocation expenses, put you in corporate housing until you got settled, and the salary is 15,000 more a year than what you were earning before. Plus you'd be eligible for annual bonuses."

Oh. Well then.

She folded the papers on her desk into a neat pile, then casually leaned back in her seat to study my reaction. "You don't have to give me an answer now. Relocation is obviously a big decision.

Go home, think about it, let me know what you decide." She rose from her seat, motioning for me to follow. "In the meantime, I'll have HR send you an official offer letter so you can look over the details."

I followed Michelle to the lobby, still stunned at the abrupt proposal. A 15,000-dollar raise? Plus bonuses? Plus free corporate housing?

Considering my alternate options (ah hem, none), I'd have to be an idiot to turn down an offer like that.

Wouldn't I?

"*Fifteen* grand?" Jasmine cheered, tossing her champagne glass in the air. "*And* corporate housing? Have you seen how nice those apartments are?"

"And annual bonuses," I added.

Jasmine locked eyes with me. "Tell me you said yes."

I glanced around the room, taking in the surroundings as I considered my response. Jasmine had taken me to the lounge bar at the W Hotel in Hollywood to celebrate, which was known as the Living Room. It was a giant spread of black-leather couches enveloping a lit stage with a red-carpeted, spiral staircase. Tonight's theme was jazz night, so we sat at a corner table and watched the band perform as burlesque dancers glided down the stairs and circled around them. I wished I had brought my camera. To anyone else it looked like an ordinary stage, but to me it was the perfect setting to shoot. Great lighting, bright colors, dancers in actions. The photographer in me always viewed my surroundings through the lens.

"Look around," I said, motioning to the scene around us. "I'd have to be an idiot not to say yes."

Before she could respond, a short Asian man wearing thick glasses and a bowtie necklace sauntered over to the table and refilled our glasses.

"Jazzy!" he yelled to Jasmine, kissing her on both cheeks like they were European. "Are you ladies enjoying yourselves?"

"We are!" Jasmine motioned to me. "Zen, this is my friend, Justine. Justine, this is Zen. He's the hotel event promoter."

Of course he was. Jasmine knew virtually every important person in the Los Angeles vicinity. He leaned over and kissed me on both cheeks.

"Lovely to meet you, Justine." Zen placed the remains of a champagne bottle on our table and walked away.

"And I'm assuming this is free," I said dryly, motioning to the bottle.

"Naturally."

I peered at her curiously. Although I had lived in LA for several years, I had never understood the whole "club promoter" logistics. "How does that work, exactly?"

"Think about it," Jasmine said in her peppy sales voice. "If you're a guy, you want to go to a trendy place with lots of hot girls. Right?"

I nodded.

"And if you're a hot girl, you can get into any happening bar in LA. So free bottle service is a great incentive to keep attractive women coming. And attractive women are a great incentive to keep the guys coming. And bring their friends. And spend lots of money in hopes of taking one of those attractive women home."

"God, you are such a sales woman."

She grinned. "So, when do you have to get back to Michelle?"

I shrugged. "She said to take my time and think it over. I figured that I'll go home, talk to my parents…"

"And Renee," she added.

I nodded hesitantly. "And Renee. Despite everything, I don't want her thinking that I moved away because of her."

"She won't. I'm sure Dylan explained everything to her. Have you heard from her?"

I shrugged. "I shut my phone off when I got here."

"You *what?*" Jasmine was one of those people who lived and

130

died by her Blackberry. I understood that being accessible was a vital part of her job, but I sometimes wished that we could have a full conversation without her checking her email 25 times.

"Since I'm only here for a few days, I want it to feel like a real vacation and not be stressed out answering angry calls from Renee," I explained. "Speaking of, if the job was already mine, then why did Sphinx fly me out here? Why didn't Michelle just call me with the details?"

Jasmine's gaze fell. "Well, I may have mentioned that you were on the fence about moving back here, so a little refresher might push you in the right direction." She smiled innocently. "Hey, I missed you, okay? And besides, Michelle thought it was a good idea."

Just then, Zen reappeared, pointing to a table to the right of the stage. "Do you ladies see who's over there?"

I squinted my eyes, scanning the VIP area, where celebrities were often spotted. "Michael Bolton?"

"No, silly!" Zen said in a high-pitched voice. "Well, him too, but I was talking about…"

"Dr. Dre," Jasmine finished. "Saw him earlier."

I looked at her, incredulous. I wouldn't notice a celebrity if he sat on my face. "How the hell did you know that?"

"Female to male ratio," she said knowingly. "Dead giveaway."

Sure enough, the table was predominantly women. All clad in very tight dresses.

I watched Zen as he walked away, floating from table to table, glowing with champagne and smiles. I leaned in toward Jasmine.

"Is Zen even his real name?"

Jasmine shot me a look like she was withholding an eye roll. "Is Zen anyone's real name?"

I couldn't help but laugh. As overindulgent, self-involved, and downright ridiculous as it was, you had to love Hollywood.

Chapter 18

Jasmine and I spent the weekend visiting all of my favorite spots in LA. On Saturday we drove up the Pacific Coast Highway and stopped in Malibu so I could photograph the ocean. I had almost forgotten how beautiful California was. Mountains next to the sand, high cliffs with gorgeous views, mixed diversities of people. I shot the sun setting into the water, the sky alternating different shades of pink and orange. I wanted to remember this feeling of inspiration every time I looked at the photos.

On Sunday, Jasmine and I went shopping at the Third Street Promenade in Santa Monica and had brunch and mimosas at our favorite roof-deck restaurant. Then we emptied our shopping bags into Jasmine's car, grabbed our towels, and hit the beach to catch some sun.

It was exactly what I needed. Somewhere warm and welcoming and carefree. A reminder of how life should be.

Well, except for the lingering familiarity of it all.

I tried not to think about David. I really did. All weekend, as we passed through the places that David and I used to frequent, I put in my best effort to push him to the back of my mind. But somehow, he was everywhere. In the line at Starbucks. At the table next to us at brunch. On the bike path at the pier.

I knew I was being ridiculous, as Los Angeles was a gigantic city and the odds of running into David were almost nonexistent. Yet I couldn't help but feel relieved that, by this time tomorrow, I'd be 3,000 miles away from him yet again.

At least for the time being.

Jasmine had planned a surprise for my last night in LA, but she refused to tell me what it was. The only insight she offered was to dress casual and be ready by 8.00.

After throwing on a pair of black skinny jeans, a sheer purple top and gold heels (which, by LA standards was still considered casual), I hopped into the passenger seat of Jasmine's Mercedes and watched out the window as we sped down Sepulveda Boulevard in the direction of Sphinx's office.

"Is this some sort of work surprise party?" I eyed her suspiciously.

"No." I could tell by her lack of hesitation that she was telling the truth. "But it is sort of a..." She searched for the right word. "*Reminiscent* place for us."

It was apparent by her shit-eating grin that I wasn't getting any more information out of her. So instead I leaned back in my seat, mentally sorting through all the places we used to frequent when we worked together. And since she invited me to a large percentage of her client happy hours, there were a lot.

However, there was one place that I sure as hell was not expecting to be our final destination.

"*Main Street?*" A rush of anxiety began to choke me. "You're taking me to David's favorite place? *Our* place?"

"Oh relax, it's a Sunday," she assured me. "He won't be here. It's dead on Sundays. Most people only come for the weekday happy hour." She pouted, her brows creasing together. "Besides, this was *our* place, too. I thought it would be fun to come here and get our usual. No one else will ever split the pretzel with me."

She did have a point. Main Street was one of our regular Sphinx after-work spots. Jasmine loved taking me there because I was always wiling to split the appetizers with her, mainly the giant Bavarian cheese-filled pretzel. It was our favorite.

"Fine," I heard myself say, even though my voice seemed disconnected from my body. I couldn't believe I was agreeing to this. I pulled down her visor mirror to make sure my red lipstick hadn't smeared. "But if you see me sprinting back to the car, you know why."

She clapped her hands together in excitement. "We can split the mini donut dessert, too! And the sweet potato tots with the spicy mayo sauce!"

I ducked my head, reluctantly stepping out of the car and following her into the bar. "You are such a foodie," I mumbled, eyeing her tiny figure. "Seriously, where do you put it?"

She linked my arm in hers, ushering me through the front door. I could feel the knots in my stomach tighten the second we set foot inside. I glanced around anxiously, scanning every bar patron with a baseball cap and muscular build that stood just above six feet tall. After a solid 30 seconds of analysis, my entire body melted into a giant wave of relief.

David Whitman was nowhere to be found.

"Happy now?" Jasmine asked, her lips pursed together to form her best "I told you so" face.

Happy didn't even begin to describe it.

After ordering a plate of sweet potato tots, raspberry-drizzled donut drops, and our usual German pretzel (all hand-picked by Jasmine, of course), I was finally starting to enjoy myself. I'd been so worried about running into David that I'd completely forgotten how much I loved Main Street. The ambiance was more welcoming than most bars in LA. A lot of local bars had a ritzy, posh-type feel, while Main Street had rock-and-roll poster-covered walls, music videos on every TV screen, and long, thin tables that resembled picnic benches. In some ways, it felt more like a friend's garage party than a bar.

Three half-eaten plates of food later, Jasmine and I were officially stuffed and ready to take on LA. We had mapped out our future, reminisced about the past (the good stuff, anyway), and caught up on all the gossip I'd missed since I'd been gone.

"I think Manuel is having an affair with Laurie," Jasmine whispered in her low, gossipy tone, like the gossipees were going to pop out from behind her and catch her in the act.

"The blonde girl in accounting? He doesn't seem like that type."

"I'm telling you. Every time I go in his office, he immediately minuses his Instant Messenger, and it's always from her."

"Maybe they're just friends."

"No way." She leaned back in her chair, crossing her arms. "I always see those little kissy face emoticons. And when his boss was on vacation, they took *very* long lunches together."

"Like how long?"

"Like four hours long."

"Ohhh." I thought about it. "I did see them leave a First Friday party together once."

"Hey!" Her eyes lit up like she'd just had an epiphany. "If you come back to Sphinx, we'll be able to go to First Friday parties together again!"

"And I can crash your client happy hours!"

"And now that you're single, we can *really* go out on the town!" She frowned. "No offense, but you're much more fun now that you don't have a boyfriend."

"I know." I hung my head sheepishly. I knew how pitiful I was when I was with David. I didn't need a reminder.

Jasmine looked at me sympathetically. "Listen, we all need to go through it at least once. That's how we learn."

"I know," I repeated. "I was... pathetic."

"Girl, pathetic doesn't even cover it. You told me once that you couldn't come to a Playboy mansion party because you guys had plans to watch some lame-ass movie and make chocolate popcorn or some shit."

"Rocky Road popcorn," I mumbled in embarrassment. "It was our thing."

"Well I guarantee if you had partied with me more often, he

wouldn't have gone anywhere." Her eyes softened. "Justine, I know you loved him. But no matter how much you adored the guy, the trick is to still maintain your own independence. Have your own life. Do your own thing. Because the second a guys feels like he completely has you, he loses interest. No one wants to feel like someone else's happiness relies solely on them."

Jasmine's advice was interrupted by our waitress, who was attempting to take one of our half-eaten plates out of the way. Jasmine shook her head sternly, moving the plate closer to her, marking her territory. The poor waitress clearly didn't know she was dealing with a girl who once left a restaurant with an entire basket of bread in her purse.

"Can I get you anything else to drink?" she asked, eyeing our water glasses.

I looked at Jasmine, who threw her hands up in surrender. "All you. I'm driving."

I skimmed the menu, considering my options. Main Street was strictly a beer and wine shop. "I'll have a glass of sangria," I said, handing the menu to the waitress.

Over the next hour, after ordering a second glass of wine, I decided it was confession time. A time that always seemed to surface with a buzz.

"I have to tell you something," I blurted out.

Jasmine raised her eyebrows, looking intrigued.

"I wasn't sure if I was going to take Michelle's offer," I admitted. "I mean, I want to, and I'd have to be crazy not to, but…"

"I know." She nodded understandably. "It would be hard to leave Renee, especially after everything you guys have been through. I'm sure a part of you is afraid that being this far away would put a strain on your friendship, especially since you're trying to rebuild it."

"But that's just it," I said. "I can't center my life around other people. I have to do this, for me. If she's my friend, then she'll always be my friend, no matter where I am." I sighed. "So I decided

I'm going to take it."

Maybe it was the wine talking, or my reminiscent state of LA bliss, but I felt as though I was seeing my life for the first time. Something about this city just felt... right. I was surrounded by love and excitement and opportunity, and all I needed was the courage to face my fears and embrace change.

"I really hope you do." Jasmine smiled proudly, but at that point, I was no longer looking at her. My gaze had frozen on the backside of a figure clad in a red shirt that stood just above six feet tall. White baseball cap. Blue jeans. Muscular arms leaning against the bar.

I would recognize that outline anywhere.

"Damn you!" I hissed, ducking my head. I slid my chair to the left so Jasmine's face was blocking mine. "I knew this was going to happen!"

"Knew what was going to happen?" Jasmine spun around, straining her neck to survey the row of bar patrons.

"Stop it!" I smacked her arm. "Turn around! He's going to see you!"

"Who's going to see me?" She was still facing the bar.

"Who do you *think*?"

Slowly, she turned back around to face me with an alarmed expression. "Red shirt?"

I nodded.

"Shit."

My heart was pounding. There was only one entrance door at Main Street, and David was standing right in front of it. It would be impossible to leave without passing right by him.

"What do I do?" I whispered.

Jasmine was silent for a moment, her eyes shifting from side to side, something she always did when weighing her options. Then her eyes landed on me, and a small smile began to spread.

"You know what you do?" she asked. "Absolutely nothing. We're going to pretend he isn't even here."

"And if he sees me?"

"Girl, look at you!" Jasmine looked me up and down. "You look smoking. He's going to take one look at you and realize what a complete idiot he is."

Oh, the panic. It was pumping through my heart, my lungs, my head. I couldn't breathe. David, the man I had been dreaming about, obsessing over, for months on end. The man who had taken up permanent residency in my brain. Here. In this very room.

"What if he tries to talk to me?" I asked. "What do I say to him?"

"Just play it cool. Pretend you've been so busy that you haven't given him a second thought."

I thought about my unemployed, uneventful life in Boston, trying to pinpoint something of interest. "Busy doing… um… what exactly?"

"Well, you could tell him that you moved back home for a while to see your family and help Renee with her baby preparations, but you just got an amazing job offer in LA and you're considering moving back here."

I tilted my head to the right, sneaking another glance at David, who was talking to two guys I didn't recognize. I couldn't believe he was really here, in front of me. My eyes traced his entire outline, the memories unraveling. His strong, toned arms that I fell asleep in every night. His hair that always smelled like pine needles. His broad, sexy shoulders.

I swallowed the last sip of my wine, attempting to drink enough courage to talk to him, but the thought was nauseating. Would he be happy to see me? Would it be an awkward, forced conversation? Would it give me the closure I needed, or just make me feel worse?

"Should I go say hi?" I asked. "Get it over with?"

"Not with that look on your face," she scolded.

"What look?"

"Like you're about to throw up."

"Oh." I frowned. "That obvious, huh?"

"Just relax," she instructed. "It'll be fine."

"I know." I swallowed. "I guess I…"

And then it happened. Just as I was attempting to steal another glance at the bar, David turned around, his eyes catching mine. My breath caught in my throat. I quickly looked away, hoping he didn't recognize me, but it was too late. He was already approaching our table.

"Justine?"

I didn't even have time to process what was happening. I couldn't look at him; the sound of his voice alone sent chills throughout my entire body. But as soon as I glanced up and our eyes locked, a complete sense of calm came over me. It was as if I knew the hardest part was about to be over.

"Hey," I greeted nonchalantly, surprised by my sudden surge of composure. "What are you doing here on a Sunday?"

"I should ask you the same thing." His eyes were glowing the way they had when we first met, and for one fleeting second, I remembered. Not the heartache, only the happiness. A time when this beautiful man was my everything. The feeling of having someone to share your life with.

Then he did something completely unexpected. After giving a quick wave to Jasmine, he leaned down, threw his arms around me, and lifted me out of my chair into a giant hug.

"It's great to see you," he said, setting me back down. He stared at me for a good ten seconds, his mouth curled in that charismatic grin I adored.

"You too."

"I thought you moved to Boston?" he asked. "I ran into one of your old coworkers a few months ago and he said you'd moved back home."

"I did," I said. "I had some things to take care of there. I just finished planning a baby shower for Renee, actually."

"Oh, wow." I searched his face for some sign of disappointment, but all I saw was surprise. "Good for her."

"Yeah, she's due next month, so I've been trying to help out as much as I can. But I was just offered a great position at Sphinx, and they want to relocate me back out here."

"That's great!" His expression was as genuine as the excitement in his voice. "Sounds like you've been busy."

I smirked at Jasmine, who was enjoying this encounter all too much. "She's been very busy," she chimed in. "I can't even get the girl to return my phone calls." She glanced down at her cell, then shot me a discreet wink. "And speaking of, I need to go make a quick call. Will you excuse me for a minute?"

We both nodded, and as soon as she was gone David slid into her seat. For the first time, I noticed his eyes were a little cloudy.

"So when do you leave?" he asked.

"I fly out tomorrow." I couldn't believe we were sitting here having a normal conversation, when our last encounter had been anything but that.

He tossed me a disappointed glance. I felt a flutter of excitement in my stomach.

"You look great," he said.

"Thank you."

We both fell silent, caught in a moment of prolonged eye contact.

"Listen," he began. "I know we have a lot to talk about. And I'm sorry I never called you. I just didn't think either one of us was ready for that conversation yet."

It was true. Although I still wasn't sure if I was ready for it. Or if I'd ever be.

"But I think we're both in a better place now," he continued. "And I really don't want to leave things the way we did."

I shuddered, thinking of the sad way he looked at me when he suggested I move out. The weight in my heart.

"Why don't we stay here and have another drink?" he proposed. "We can catch up."

I paused, chewing on my bottom lip hesitantly.

"Are you staying with Jasmine?" he asked.

I nodded.

"Culver City's not that far. I can get you a cab later."

I leaned forward, studying his eyes. He was definitely drunk. I didn't care. I needed this.

"Okay," I agreed. "But I have a flight to catch tomorrow, so just one drink. That's it."

Even though David nodded in agreement, I knew that neither of us believed that for a second.

Chapter 19

"Are you crazy?"

"Jasmine…"

"No, seriously. Are you out of your mind? You're going to stay here with him? The guy who broke your heart? The one you've spent the past six months trying to get over?"

I had followed Jasmine into the bathroom to plead my case about staying for another drink with David, to which she was not thrilled.

"You do realize this is the same guy that almost ruined your relationship with your best friend, right?"

"It wasn't all his fault. I was there, too. It's just as much my fault as it is his."

"And now you're making excuses for him."

"It's just one drink."

She rolled her eyes. "It's never just one drink, and you know it."

"I know," I sighed. "But I need the closure. I'll never be able to move on without it."

Jasmine was silent for a minute, then nodded as though my explanation had met her acceptance.

"I'm just looking out for you," she said softly. "The guy cheated on your best friend and went after you, and then once he had you, kicked you out. He's not a good person, Justine."

"I just don't want to leave things the way we did," I explained. "And neither does he. I think if we talk about everything, it'll help me get on with my life. It always felt… unfinished."

"Okay, okay," she said, giving in. "Just promise me you'll call me if you need a ride later." She glanced down at my purse. "I know your cell phone is on vacation mode, but you did bring it with you, right?"

I nodded.

"Good. And you have a flight to catch tomorrow, so you better not be out too late."

"Yes, mom," I joked.

She grinned. "And promise me one more thing – you won't do anything stupid."

"Of course not."

The words sounded believable, and I really, truly wanted to believe them. But deep down, I couldn't help but worry that they didn't have any truth to them at all.

As predicted, I did not stick to the one-drink rule. Unless you count half of a beer pitcher as one drink.

For the rest of the night, David and I caught up on everything that had occurred over the past six months. It wasn't anything of excitement really, just small everyday tidbits. David had received a promotion at work, bought a new car, joined a softball league. I exaggerated the details of my life in Boston, romanticizing my band photo shoots, talking myself up to be some glamorous nightlife photographer that hung out at rock shows in the city with Renee. Then I put on a dramatic display of indecision as I discussed leaving my fabulous life in Boston to return to LA. David ate up every word, listening with sparks in his eyes, like he had found the girl he'd once fallen in love with. It was laughable really. He thought I was some hotshot career woman in demand, when really I was an unemployed loser who'd spent the last six months curled up on my couch crying over him.

At half-past midnight, the bar lights came on for last call, and I realized that David and I still hadn't touched on any subjects that pertained to our relationship. I felt a slight pang of disappointment, realizing that maybe it was too late. We had wasted the last two hours making small talk, and I didn't have an ounce of closure to walk away with.

Reading my mind, David looked up at the lights and turned to me with a hesitant look. "I know it's late, but I do have a lot I want to talk to you about."

"Me too."

He glanced around the bar. "This place is closing soon, but… I have some beer at my place if you want to talk there?"

Just the thought of being at David's house made my hands start to shake. "I don't know if that's a good idea."

"Well if it makes you feel any better, I promise to be a *perfect gentleman*."

We both burst out laughing at our former inside joke. God, it was so hard to stay mad at him. I knew the logistics. I should've hated him. I wanted to hate him. But as I looked over at that face I had once lost myself in, there was a part of me that couldn't blame him. You can't help falling out of love with someone. The same way you can't help falling in love with someone. Like I did.

"Okay," I said. "But my flight is at noon tomorrow, so I really can't stay too long."

My third false promise of the night.

They say that scents and songs are two of the most powerful memory-inducers that exist. After David and I split, there was a period where every song reminded me of him, but fortunately his scent was on the opposite side of the country.

As soon as I set foot inside his apartment, it was like entering a time warp. Not just because it look identical to the last time I'd seen it, but because the scent almost knocked the wind out of me. A rush of emotions swept through me instantly – love, loss, confusion, hurt – and, for a brief moment, I almost turned around and bolted.

Then there was the visual effect. Because at one time this had been *my* house, too. My couch. My table. My bed. *Our* bed.

As I looked around, inhaling my past, I realized this probably wasn't the best idea. But it was too late. I was here. And I wasn't leaving without my closure.

David grabbed two beers from the fridge, handed one to me, then sat on the opposite end of the couch, his body facing mine. He seemed genuinely at ease, almost as if the breakup had never existed. Something about his demeanor made me relax a bit.

"I'm really sorry about what happened with Renee," he said, launching right into it. "You two had been friends for a long time and I never should've interfered. I'm glad to hear you're in a good place again, though."

"We are," I said. "But it wasn't all your fault. I'm just as much to blame."

"Nah." He shook his head. "You told me no a thousand times and I wouldn't hear it." He looked sad, remorseful. "But I want you to know that I only did it because of how strongly I felt at the time. I really did love you, Justine."

"I know," I said. And I did. Although there was an angry part of me that wanted to believe it had all been a game to him, I knew that wasn't entirely true. The connection we had, the emotions. You couldn't fake that.

"I feel badly about the way I treated you," he continued. "That was never my intention."

"So what happened?" I had to ask. It was the one thing I never understood. I assumed it was because I had lost my independence, become boring, routine. But I needed to hear it from him.

He let out a noise that sounded like a half sigh, half contemplative moan. Several times he started to reply, then stopped himself, like he was trying to pinpoint the exact reason why our relationship fell apart.

"I know I changed," I said. "I became dependent on you, and I'm sure that wasn't easy."

"That was part of it," he agreed. "But I also started thinking about Renee a lot, probably because I never really had a chance to get over our relationship since you and I jumped right into one. I never felt the breakup, I just moved on. Then, all of a sudden, everything caught up with me and I kept thinking about how much I'd hurt her. I felt so bad that I decided I had to apologize." When he spoke, he couldn't meet my eyes. "And yes, at the time, you had lost your independence, which was something Renee had never done, and probably would never do, knowing her. And I began second-guessing our relationship, and more importantly, whether or not I give up on relationships too easily in general."

"So you went to see her," I said.

"So I went to see her," he repeated. I'd already heard the story from Renee; how David had showed up unannounced at her apartment to make amends, but hearing it from David's perspective felt completely different.

"I went to Boston, as I'm assuming you already know," he continued. "And she obviously wasn't thrilled to see me. But I'm glad I got the chance to see that she's happy now, and that I got to apologize to her face to face. Much like I need to do now. With you."

David's remorse gave me mixed emotions. It made it easier to let go of my resentment, but harder to let go of the love that still lingered. I couldn't help but wonder if he was apologizing to ease his conscience, or if he still loved me, too.

"You know, I'll be honest, I thought you were going to take the breakup pretty hard, but…" David broke into a grin. "Look at you! You look incredible. It's great to hear you're doing so well. You never cease to amaze me, Justine."

I forced a smile and took a sip of my beer so I wouldn't have to look at him. I felt like such a fraud. If he only knew that I spent my spare time (which was, essentially, all of my time) hiding pictures of him and staring at my silent phone and reading meditation books to get over him, he would… well, he would be pretty glad he broke up with me.

"Yeah, things are coming together," I said. "As much as I love my friends and family back home, I really miss LA."

And you, I thought.

"What's not to miss?" David disappeared into the kitchen, returning with a familiar- looking bottle. "After living in LA, I don't understand how you could live anywhere else."

"Um, excuse me, what is that?" I asked, pointing to the bottle of Fireball whiskey in his hand.

He tossed me a mischievous glance. "For old times' sake," he said, pouring us each a shot.

"No way." I held my hands up in protest. "I do not want to be hung over on an airplane. And isn't that how we got into trouble in the first place?"

David feigned a hurt expression, handing me one of the glasses. "Oh come on, it wasn't that bad, was it? We had some good times, right?"

I took the glass from him hesitantly. We did have some good times. That I could agree. I just wasn't sure if all the pain was worth it.

I peered into the glass, swirling the liquid around, contemplating. After a few moments, I brought the glass to my lips and downed the shot in one gulp.

Four shots later, David and I were in the exact same position we'd been in that first night. It was like déjà vu. We talked, we laughed, and we somehow ended up sitting way too close to each other on the couch. I watched his crazed eyes studying me, looking at me in a way that had now become a distant memory. I felt his hand not-so-accidentally graze my leg every time I said something funny. But before it could go any further, I moved away from him, separating myself from the same spell I had once fallen under.

"This has been really fun," I said, standing up. "But I should go."

His face fell and a jolt of exhilaration sparked in me. He didn't

147

want me to leave. I wasn't sure to what extent, but something told me there was a part of him that still cared.

"Don't go," he said, rising to his feet. "It feels like you just got here."

"David, it's…" I glanced at the clock. "It's almost three in the morning! I have to be at the airport at ten!"

"So stay," he said in a low voice.

"I can't."

He moved closer to me. My heart was in my throat. He lowered his head, searching for my eyes, but I couldn't look at him. I had to stay strong.

"Stay," he repeated. I felt his voice more than I heard it. It was reaching out, drawing me in. "I'll drive you back in the morning."

It would've been so easy, to fall back into his arms, our bed, the familiarity. But what did I hope to gain from it? Closure? Another heartbreak? A second chance? I didn't know what to think, because I didn't know what he was thinking.

"What do you want?" I asked in a small voice.

He knelt down so his head was facing up at me. I had no choice but to meet his eyes. I knew what I must've looked like – nervous, confused, terrified. But David was the exact opposite. His eyes were full of yearning, lust, desire.

And at that moment, I knew it would take everything in me to resist him.

"You," he whispered. "I've always wanted you."

I didn't even try to fight it. I just surrendered, letting him take my lips in his, embracing his body as it locked around mine. I put my hands behind his neck, tasted the cinnamon on his tongue, smelled the nostalgic scent of his hair. I felt myself relax against him, allowing his arms to curve around my waist, his hands running down the side of my body.

He guided me in the direction of the bedroom, but I felt like I was floating. I was surprised to open my eyes and find we were in a different room than where we'd started.

David removed his shirt, then mine, pulling my hips into his. "Tell me what you want," he said, his eyes burning into mine.

It was a game we'd always played. Every time we had sex, we'd ask each other to choose a position. And we gave a different answer every time, because we vowed to never become one of those couples with a boring sex life.

"Tell me," he repeated, removing my bra, taking my breasts in his mouth.

We fell onto the bed together, our limbs interlocked, fumbling to get our pants off. I felt him hard against me, his body pressed against mine, grinding in a rhythmic pattern.

"You know what I want," I murmured. He knew my favorite position. The only way I'd ever been able to orgasm was if I was on top.

He pulled me on to him, tossing my red-lace thong onto the floor. He slipped his fingers inside me, running them in a circular motion as his tongue made its way to the curve of my neck.

When I couldn't take it anymore, I moved downward, leaving a small trail of kisses from his chest to his bellybutton. He moaned as I took him inside of me, running my tongue up and down, sucking hard. He reached down and cupped my breasts in his hands, moaning louder as he pushed against the back of my throat.

Slowly, I moved back up and straddled him, easing him inside of me. At that moment, it dawned on me that I hadn't had sex in over six months. And the last time I had, I'd been in this exact same place with this exact same person.

He gripped my thighs as I moved over him, and I watched his stomach muscles flex and contract. I couldn't believe this was real. Maybe the alcohol had suppressed my emotions, but being here, with him, felt like a dream.

I lowered myself onto him, my face in his hair. God he smelled so good. Like fabric softener and cinnamon and sex. His hands found their way to my ass, pushing me harder against him, until I felt everything inside of me explode. I cried out, shuddering, slowing my pace to a halt.

David flipped me onto my back and slipped himself back into me, thrusting faster. He leaned down and kissed me hard, then pulled back, picking up the pace. I watched him as he moved, still too stunned to comprehend what was happening. What would happen.

He pulled himself out, finishing with a long, quivering sigh as he stroked himself onto my stomach. Then he collapsed next to me, rolling onto his side, facing me. Even in the dark, I could see him staring, with a question on his face that I couldn't quite read.

I lay awake for a long time after he fell asleep, wondering, contemplating, trying to make sense of it all. I had come here for closure and left with nothing. The only thing I'd done was give David yet another piece of my heart that I'd never get back.

Chapter 20

I awoke the next morning in a frenzy, partially because I only had an hour to get my things from Jasmine's and get to the airport, and partially because David was nowhere to be found. I breathed a sigh of relief when I heard the sound of the shower running. Ah, yes. It was Monday. He didn't leave; he just had to get ready for work.

I lay there for a few minutes, my head in the pillow, breathing in the scent of him. There was something about his hair that had always smelled like sex to me. I used to love the way it lingered on the pillows, in the sheets.

My nostalgia came to a halt as soon as I heard the shower water turn off, as I had no clue how today was going to go. Was last night the closure I was looking for – one final hurrah? Did he regret it? Or did he realize he still had feelings for me and wanted to work on things again?

I thought back to his words. *You. I've always wanted you.* I remembered the way he looked at me, how intently he listened when I spoke about my life. The way he begged me to stay.

Judging from last night, it definitely seemed like things were headed in the right direction. Maybe this was supposed to happen. Maybe we needed some time apart so I could find myself again, and now that I had a job offer in LA everything would work out.

At least this was what I thought until David walked into the bedroom looking like he'd seen a ghost.

"Hey," he said, appearing visibly uncomfortable. "You're awake."

I sat up and watched as he threw on a white polo shirt and a pair of khakis. Then he came over and sat down at the end of the bed.

"Justine, I…" He let out a long breath. "I had *a lot* to drink last night. And I did want to apologize to you, but this…" He motioned to his bed. To *me*, naked in his bed. "This was not supposed to happen."

Ouch. I felt like I'd been punched in the stomach and he hadn't even finished what he was about to say. Everything inside of me tightened as I braced myself for what was coming.

"I know," I said, trying to lighten the mood. "I wasn't planning on this either. But you seemed like you were having a good time."

"I was," he insisted. "It was great seeing you. But…"

"So maybe, when I move back, we can get together and see how things go. If you want." I shrugged. "Think about it. I won't be back for at least a month anyway."

"That's just it." He lowered his head into his hands. "Justine, I'm… I'm engaged."

Everything inside of me turned to stone. It was worse than when Vincent told me he was married. It was almost as bad as Renee walking in on David and me. It was like my life was one long nightmare that never ended.

"Is this a joke?" I gripped the sheets to my chest, suddenly feeling completely foolish that I was naked in his bed. The bed that he shared with his *fiancé*. "Are you kidding me?"

The look on his face indicated that clearly, he was not.

"David, we've been broken up for *six months*. How could you possibly be engaged?"

He massaged his temples with his index fingers, his eyes trained on the floor. "It all happened so fast. I met her right after I saw Renee. I know it sounds crazy, but it just felt so right. I mean, haven't you ever…?"

His sentence came to a halt once he saw the death look I was giving him.

"Right. I'm sorry." He winced. "Justine, I never wanted to hurt you. It just happened, and she's…"

"What's her name?" My voice was cold.

He squinted at me. "Do you really want to do this?"

"What's her name?" I repeated, harsher this time.

"Fiona."

It figured. Even her name was beautiful.

"Where's she from?"

"Justine…"

My lips pressed into a straight line. I crossed my arms, making it clear I wasn't moving until he answered my questions.

He ran his hand along the back of his neck. "Australia."

"Australia," I said in a mocking tone. "Isn't that sweet. Where did you meet her?"

"On a photo shoot for *Pace*. She's a…"

"Let me guess. She's a model."

He nodded.

My lips curled into a sneer. "How cliché."

David slowly moved his head to the right, looking at me with scared eyes. It was as though everything in me had frozen. All the burning love I'd had for him, even up until minutes before, was gone. I was hollow. Empty.

I rose from the bed, allowing him one last view of my naked body before putting my clothes back on. I stared him down as I dressed, watching his unease increase, enjoying every second. Once I was fully clothed, I stood in front of him, blocking his ability to avoid me.

"One last question and then I'll go," I said. "Why her?"

His brow furrowed as he tried to think of a reply. "I don't know. I've never met anyone like her. She's fascinating. She's traveled all over the world. She's really cultured, and passionate, and…"

"Okay." I held up my hand to stop him. That was all I needed to hear. I guess I'd finally got my closure after all, just not in the way I'd planned.

I walked into the living room, threw on my shoes, and grabbed my purse. Before I was at the door, I heard David call out after me.

"Justine," he said. "Do you, um… do you still need a ride?"

Because of the time difference, I landed in Boston just before 9pm that night. I powered on my phone as soon as the plane hit the runway, and breathed a heavy sign of relief when I saw two voicemails from Renee. In the first voicemail, she cried and apologized for overreacting about the shower, blaming her behavior on pregnancy hormones. In the second voicemail, she was concerned that she still hadn't heard from me and asked me to call her as soon as I could.

After a seemingly endless trail of suitcases, escalators, elevators, and parking garage levels, I drove straight to Renee's without even calling. Quincy was only a ten-minute drive from the airport, and knowing the night owl Renee was, she was most likely still up.

As soon as she saw me at her front door, Renee burst into tears and threw her arms around me. I began to cry in return, but for a much different reason.

"It's okay," I said, stroking her back. "I'm not mad."

"I am such an ass," she sobbed. "You put so much effort into finding those decorations, and look at how I treated you."

"Well, it's sort of understandable," I sympathized. "You know, considering."

She broke away, forcing a laugh, and led me inside. Sitting on her living-room sofa was Beth, clearly amused at our display of affection.

"Hi," I greeted, waving to Beth. I looked around the room. "Where's Dylan?"

"At Andy's," Renee said. "Guys' night. Beth's keeping me company." She eyed me suspiciously as I sat down on the loveseat. "Where have you been, anyway? I've been calling you for days."

"I just got back from LA. I landed about a half hour ago, got

154

your message, and came right here."

"What were you doing in LA?" Beth asked.

As I opened my mouth to tell them about the interview and my weekend with Jasmine, my mind was instantly flooded with images of David. David telling me he wanted me. David asking me to stay. David's mouth all over me. David and his fiancé, making love in the same bed that we'd just shared.

And then I burst into tears.

It was like a pipe had opened and the tears wouldn't stop. They just flowed with each emerging memory, an endless emotional current. Renee and Beth exchanged concerned looks, both suspecting the same thing.

"Tell me you didn't go to see him," Renee said.

I shook my head, wiping my cheeks with my hands. Beth disappeared into the bathroom, returning with a box of tissues. I took them from her and dabbed at my eyes.

"I went for a job interview," I explained. "Sphinx made me a really great offer for an event manager position."

"You're *leaving*?" Renee's eyes filled up again.

"Nothing's definite yet. I'm just weighing my options."

I had to downplay how close I was to accepting Sphinx's offer, as I didn't want to upset Renee any more in her hormonal state, nor did I want her thinking I was leaving because of what had happened between us.

"I spent the weekend with Jasmine," I continued. "And last night, we ran into David."

I could barely even speak his name, let alone the rest of the story. The words came out like I was being choked. *Wanted to catch up... one more drink... his house... apologized... closure... stay... couldn't stop... next morning... engaged...*

I cried and cried as the two listened in disbelief.

"Ouch," Beth said, cringing.

"He is such an ass," Renee scoffed, shaking her head. "I guess I shouldn't be surprised but... cheating on his fiancé? And not telling you about her? That's pretty low, even for him."

"Justine, listen," Beth said. "I know it hurts now, but this is exactly what you need."

"She's right," Renee agreed. "If there was even a small possibility of you two getting back together, you never would've got over him."

"I know," I said, even though David's engagement felt like the last thing in the world that was a positive thing. But they were right. Clearly, if David was willing to cheat on someone he was supposed to spend the rest of his life with, he wasn't the person I thought he was.

"And you know what's going to happen, right?" Beth said. "If he's already cheating on this girl, there's no way in hell they're going to last. Which means the minute they break up, he's going to do exactly what he did with Renee. He's going to call you and beg for forgiveness and by then you're going to be long over him."

A week ago, I couldn't imagine being long over David. Now, I felt one step closer.

"Men are lazy," Beth continued. "They'd rather crawl back to something comfortable than invest the energy into looking for something new."

"Fact," Renee said.

"And honestly, as much as Renee is going to disagree with me on this one, I think going to that interview in LA is one of the smartest decisions you've made in a long time." Beth tossed a regretful glance at Renee, who was frowning at her. "If you're not happy here, then you need a change. Get a job you love, move on with your life."

"She can find a job here," Renee argued. "It takes time. She doesn't need to take the first offer she gets."

"If it's a good offer, then maybe she should," Beth shot back. "It doesn't have to be forever. She could move out there for a year or two, gain some experience, and then use that experience to land a job here if she misses home and wants to move back."

"You guys don't have to talk about me like I'm not here," I said.

"I've thought about all of this already. But the job isn't the only reason I'm considering it. To be honest, I really loved living in LA. I love the weather and the culture and how inspiring it is for my photography. The only thing I hate, besides leaving everyone here, is that everything reminds me of David."

"Well you can't let a guy ruin a great opportunity for you," Beth said. "And Justine…" She paused, and the judgmental tone in her voice told me I wasn't going to like what she was about to say. "You should really consider seeing a therapist to figure out why you always pick the wrong men."

"I don't *always* pick the wrong men," I snapped. "You can't help who you fall in love with. If you could, do you think I would've chosen to fall in love with Renee's boyfriend?"

"Well, there's something drawing you to the same type of guys," Beth said. "Renee said that before David you were dating some guy who was married."

I felt everything in me tighten in defense. "I didn't know he was married!" I yelled. "I thought he was a nice guy!"

"Exactly," Beth said, in her critical, matter-of-fact tone. "There's something in you that's drawn to unavailable men, whether you realize it or not."

"That is so not fair," I argued. "You can't control your feelings. I tried like hell to resist David, but…"

"But you didn't," Beth interjected. "Regardless of how you felt about this guy, that should've been a pretty big red flag that not only was this guy willing to cheat on his girlfriend, but he was willing to cheat on her with her best friend."

It sounded so stupid, hearing it from an outsider's perspective. Of course, that was a red flag. To anyone else, the logical decision was perfectly clear. But love wasn't logical. Beth didn't know David or the connection we had. No one did. It was impossible to put into words.

"You don't understand," I mumbled.

"I do," Renee said, her lips twisting into a small smile. "I know

157

how David is. He's extremely charming and extremely manipulative. When he wants something, he doesn't give up. And if you were in love with him and he knew it, it was only a matter of time." She looked at me sympathetically. "I also know you don't fall in love very easily. In all the years I've known you, I've never seen you this upset over a guy."

I nodded, grateful for the momentary save.

"Okay, so you were head over heels for the guy, but once he had you, he broke up with you, told you to move out, and never called you again." Beth cocked an eyebrow. "And then, the first time you see him, you go home with him?" Her eyes narrowed. "Come on, Justine. You should've told him to fuck off. Have some respect for yourself."

My blood had officially come to a boil. "Oh, I'm sorry, I didn't realize you were the relationship expert here," I hissed. "You and Eddie have broken up... exactly how many times now? And you call that a good relationship?" I tossed her a condescending look. "Sounds like settling to me."

"Settling, huh? Is that why he bought me this?" Beth smiled smugly, raising her left hand to expose a shiny emerald-cut diamond on her ring finger.

Renee glared at her. "That was mean," she said in low voice. "She's going through a hard time, Beth. You don't have to rub your happiness in her face."

"But it's okay for her to say that Eddie and I are settling for each other?" Beth squared her shoulders, rising from her chair. "God, Renee. She can do whatever she wants to you and you still stick up for her."

As I watched Beth storm out the door, I couldn't help but feel a sting of jealousy. Even hypercritical, outspoken Beth Broadley had found someone who loved her. It seemed like everyone around me had someone to spend their lives with, and I was just floating around in a pool of unavailable men, searching to find unattainable love in the last place I should be looking.

Chapter 21

The internet was an evil, evil invention. A cruel, cackling abundance of unnecessary knowledge, ready and waiting, at your disposal. A place where, in less than an hour's time, you could find anything and everything you'd ever wanted to know about someone. And even things you didn't want to know.

Her name was Fiona Marsden. She'd grown up in Melbourne, Australia, and now lived in West Hollywood. She was 25, five foot nine, blonde and beautiful. Not exotic-beautiful in the way you'd imagine a model to be, more of a girl-next-door beautiful. Bright, round, blue eyes, waist-long hair, wide smile. It was easy to see what David liked about her. She had that carefree glow of youth and innocence. I imagined her smiling at strangers in the subway, reading a book on a park bench in some foreign country.

It'd been rather easy to find her information. All I had to do was find the edition of *Pace* that had launched around the time they'd met. There she was on page 36, modeling a fitness clothing line at a sporting event that *Pace* had sponsored. And then, once I had her name, the beautiful internet directed me to the rest of her life.

Surprisingly, as I trolled through her modeling portfolio, searching for something, any sort of flaw, I just couldn't hate her. She looked… nice. Sweet. Like someone who sure-as-hell deserved a lot better than David.

Most of her Facebook photos were private, which was a good thing because as much as I didn't want to see her and David together, if it was there, it would be impossible not to look. Every day. And show people. And look again. And drive myself insane.

Thankfully, David didn't have a Facebook profile. Another boost to my sanity.

Of course, there was the vengeful part of me that wanted to email her and tell her that her fiancé was a cheating asshole, but I knew better. She'd figure it out on her own, in time. Hopefully before it was too late.

As I looked through her photos one last time, a feeling of sadness came over me. I was certain that once I saw who she was, I'd hate her, but instead I just felt sad for her. Because at one time, I had been her. And one day, she would be me. I would never wish that upon anyone.

Back to the book I went. As much as I hated to admit it, Beth's words had really gotten to me. The problem was, I was too stubborn for therapy. I was more of a solve-my-own-issues type of girl.

The next chapter in *My Kick-Ass Life* talked about the conscious and subconscious minds, and how our upbringing and past experiences affected the person we were today. As I delved into the pages, trying to figure out the cause of my faltered love life, I came up empty. My parents were happily married. I had a good relationship with my father. I'd never suffered a traumatic experience.

So, then, why did I keep attracting the wrong people into my life? Was it just a case of bad luck?

When all else fails, make a list.

I slammed the book shut, grabbed a notebook and pen, and began to jot down a list of every man I'd ever slept with. Only this time, instead of a to-do list, it was an already-did list.

Been There, Done That – The List: by Justine Sterling

Tommy Boyd – High-school bad boy. Now known as inmate Boyd.

Dan Pearson – Sophomore-year one-night-stand. Weirdly obsessed with feet.

Alex Walker – First love slash jealous lunatic.

Sam McCormick – AKA "the minuteman."

Rob Palermo – Italian. Adorable. Couldn't be faithful to save his life.

Ben Jameson – Booty call turned boyfriend. Didn't think that could happen.

Ace – Miami fling. Didn't know his real name. Didn't care.

Mark Wheeler – Great boyfriend. Total bore. Favorite pastimes: romantic comedies, missionary position. Yawn.

Matt Romero – First rebound sex. Sucked.

Jesse Minolt –First college fling. Small.

Chris Lena – Really sweet. Really polite. Really should've told me he had three children before we slept together.

Brad Chapelle – Cancun fling involving a lot of Tequila and a tire swing.

Johnny Queen – Lead singer in a band. Never again.

David Whitman – Liar. Cheater. Soul thief.

And there they were, the fourteen men under scrutiny. I scoured the entire list, looking for some sort of explanation or common denominator. Had I always had bad taste in men? When did it start? Had I been attracting the wrong type of guy all along?

If they were all David Whitman replicas – unfaithful, dishonest, manipulative – then, yes, I would have a serious problem. But even though some of them may have had jealousy issues, or commitment issues, or lacked in the bedroom department, most of them were actually pretty decent guys.

Confession: I've never slept with a man that I didn't love in some way.

It was true. I'd even kept in touch with my Cancun fling. I wasn't exactly a vision of monogamy, but my heart was usually in the right place.

After a bit more analysis, I put the list away and resumed my place in the book. My past was, for the most part, fine. Sure, I had some things I had to work on, but so did everyone. I didn't need a therapist to tell me that.

"This is going to be so much fun!"

Renee's house-hunting expedition: day two.

I frowned at her. "How do I always get conned into these things? Shouldn't Dylan be here?"

"Well considering Dylan isn't Walter's biggest fan, I think he wants to minimize their time together. I'm lucky he even agreed to keep Walter as our agent." Her eyebrows creased into a straight line. "And since when do I have to *con* you into hanging out with a gorgeous guy?"

"Okay, a) I am in no position to be dating right now, and b) he has a girlfriend."

"Whatever." She shooed me with her hand. "Most relationships don't last anyway."

"Says the girl who's getting married," I retorted. "Do you think you guys will have a problem getting a mortgage approval? Since you're both self-employed?"

"It isn't ideal, but you wouldn't believe how much money Dylan saved when he was working in construction."

"I would think if he's using his life savings on a house, he'd want to be here."

"He will be. I'm just going to look at the ones I liked online and narrow it down to a few. Then we'll look at those together and agree on one."

It seemed sad to me, that Renee was house-hunting with me instead of her fiancé. But then I realized that was how their relationship worked. Renee was too independent to be with a needy guy that did everything with her. And musicians weren't exactly the most available people, so they couldn't have a needy partner either. It worked for her, but I'd never want it for myself. I liked having a counterpart.

"Walter should be here any minute," Renee said, looking at her watch.

The first stop of the day was a colonial house in Medford. The plan was to start north of the city and work our way south. Renee had researched dozens of houses within a fifteen-mile radius of Quincy and narrowed it down to three for today's hunt.

I gazed up at the house, which looked like what they referred to in California as a "tall skinny." It had two floors and a very narrow shape, but not much of a yard. I tried to picture Renee and Dylan starting their lives here as a family, but the thought still seemed strange to me. Renee seemed too young to be mom.

I looked over just in time to see Walter's black Audi pull up and park along the curb. As he stepped out of the car, I noticed he was dressed much more casually than the last time I'd seen him, in faded jeans and an army green button-up coat that brought out the gold in his eyes.

"Hey," he greeted, making his way to the porch, where Renee and I were standing. "Sorry I'm late."

"It's okay," Renee said. "We haven't been waiting long."

Walter unlocked the front door and led us inside, giving us a full tour of the house. I was immediately drawn to the living room's built-in bookshelves and brick fireplace, but the room itself was a bit on the smaller side. The kitchen made up for it, though; an enormous open space with granite countertops, stainless-steel appliances, a bar, and a bright, open dining room attached.

All three bedrooms were upstairs, and I loved the way the cathedral ceilings dipped down and gave them a loft-type feel. I studied Renee's face, trying to gauge her reaction and see if it matched mine.

"So what do you think?" Walter asked, before leading us back downstairs.

"I like it," Renee said, with a nod of approval. "The kitchen's my favorite."

163

"Yeah, they remodeled the whole place recently," he said. "You can tell everything's new."

"I just wish it had more of a yard," she admitted, frowning. "And that the location was a little closer."

"Medford's not too far," I said.

"Don't you Bostonians pronounce it med-fid?" Walter joked.

I smiled shyly. "I think I lost the accent when I lived in California."

"Careful," he said, grinning. "If you stick around too long, you might pick it back up." He looked at Renee. "Well, the other two places are closer to you, right?"

Renee nodded. "South Boston and Quincy. Dylan and I want to stay a little closer south since our families are there, but I really liked this house too. It's a great price, and the size is perfect."

"Well, let's go check out the other two and see what you think," Walter proposed. "And if you want, we can grab some lunch afterward."

Renee snuck me a glance, wiggling her eyebrows. I stifled a laugh.

"I think that sounds great," Renee agreed.

The second house on our destination list was a light-blue, two-story in south Boston. It had a wraparound covered porch, a bright-red door, and yellow flowers lining the front yard. I loved it before we even stepped inside.

As soon as Walter opened the door, I was surrounded by bright, luminous rays of light. Large picture windows and sparkling hardwood floors welcomed us from all directions. The entrance hallway contained an old wooden staircase and French double doors that led to the living room.

The kitchen wasn't as modern or spacious as the house in Medford, but still a decent size and condition. The bedrooms were all equipped with high ceilings and equally as bright as the living room, with oversized windows lining each wall.

The second floor housed a back staircase that led to an enormous, fenced-in backyard and another small back patio. I could see Renee and Dylan hosting cookouts here, Dylan strumming his acoustic guitar on the porch, Renee setting up an outside bar to serve drinks. It definitely had potential.

"So…" Walter began, looking at Renee expectantly.

I didn't even have to guess. The look on Renee's face gave it away completely.

"I *love* it," she said, clasping her hands together. "It's very urban but has lots of classic charm to it. Artsy yet modern."

"Agreed," I said. "And you could have some kick-ass barbecues in this yard."

"That's what I was thinking!" Renee exclaimed.

"Alright then," Walter said, clearly happy that Renee had an ideal prospect. "Two down, one to go." He looked from Renee to me. "Do you want to take my car and we can stop for lunch after?"

"Sure," we agreed in unison.

And with that, we were off to destination number three.

The house in Quincy proved to be very similar to the south Boston house, only a less-appealing version. For one, Renee was not too keen on the wall coloring, seeing as though every room was a different color. The living room was painted canary yellow, the kitchen pale pink, the bedrooms fluorescent green and orange. You'd think the previous owners were colorblind.

Despite the similarities between both houses – light-blue exterior, two floors, fireplace, large backyard – the biggest deal-breaker was the kitchen. The wooden cabinets were outdated, and the floors matched the ugly brick tile on the walls. All in all, it seemed like more work than Renee was willing to put in.

Once the house-hunting was complete, Walter took us to lunch at a diner in Harvard Square that was best known for their burgers and beer garden. The ambiance was that of a true diner – black-and-white checkered floors, red-leather booths, old records prominently displayed on the walls.

"Justine, why don't you sit next to Walter?" Renee smirked, clutching her stomach. "You know, since I need all the room I can get."

I rolled my eyes behind Water's back. The girl who thought I had bad taste in men, trying to hook me up with a guy who had a girlfriend.

After relaying our orders to the waitress – veggie wrap for me, grilled cheese for Renee, burger with waffle fries for Walter – Renee and Walter launched into a real-estate debate.

"So, ideally, if you could pick anywhere, where would be your number-one place to buy a house?" Walter asked.

"It would be great to live in the Allston/Brighton area, since that's where most of the venues are that Dylan plays," Renee said. "But there are no affordable houses there. Since our families are on the south shore and Dylan works in the city, Quincy and south Boston are ideal because they're sort of a halfway point."

"Speaking of Southie," Walter said, looking at me. "I think that apartment you liked might be taken. Someone put a deposit on it last week."

"That's okay, Justine's moving back to California anyway," Renee sang, sticking out her tongue at me.

"Really?" Walter raised his eyebrows.

"I never said I was moving back," I argued. "But I did get a job offer that I'm considering."

"Relocation isn't an easy decision," Walter sympathized. "My father wants me to move to Boston to oversee the new office, but my girlfriend doesn't want to move here."

"And how is your girlfriend?" Renee asked in an obviously loud voice, putting extra emphasis on the word "girlfriend." It was a miracle she never took up acting in LA.

"She's doing well," Walter answered, completely oblivious to Renee's obnoxiousness. "But the traveling does put a strain on our relationship sometimes."

166

"Told you," Renee mouthed when he wasn't looking.

"Well, she should really be more supportive of your career," she quipped. I almost choked on my water.

Just then, our waitress arrived at the table with our lunches, setting the plates down in front of us. "Do you need anything else?" she asked.

"Just some ketchup for the fries would be great," Walter said. "Do you girls need anything?"

It was at that moment, as Renee and I both shook our heads, that I noticed how truly thoughtful Walter was. Every time our waitress checked on us, he would make sure that both Renee and I were content before sending her away. Every time she bought a condiment to the table, Walter acted like she'd given him a million dollars. Even with looks like his, he had zero sense of entitlement; he lived in a constant state of appreciation. It gave me hope, just knowing that someone like him existed. There were plenty of good guys like Walter out there. And the sooner I stopped sulking, the sooner I'd find one of my own.

Chapter 22

As luck would have it, we still managed to surprise Renee on the day of her shower. Dylan had told her it was going to be the following weekend at his mother's house, so she was completely caught off guard when she walked into her own parents' house and found 50 of her closest friends and family members waiting for her, surrounded by an assortment of baby-music memorabilia.

I'll admit, I was nervous of seeing Beth, since this was our first face-to-face encounter since the night at Renee's house. The two of us had pretty much avoided each other all morning, as we each went about our business of setting up and making sure that everything was in place before Renee arrived.

After the big surprise, everyone gathered around the kitchen table, snacking on appetizers and mixing cocktails, until it was time for Renee to open the presents.

Before following everyone into the living room, I wandered over to the bar to mix myself a mimosa. When I turned back around, Beth was standing there. Our eyes caught for a moment, both of us silent, until she flashed me an apologetic smile.

"Hey," she said, holding up her glass. "Mind topping me off?"

"Sure." I lifted the bottle, filling her champagne flute to the top.

She set the glass down on the counter and turned to face me. "Listen, I'm sorry about the other night," she said. "Sometimes

I say things when I'm trying to be helpful, but it usually comes out the wrong way."

"I know," I said. Beth had always been that way. She liked to offer constructive criticism, but there was a fine line between being diplomatic and being rude that she hadn't quite mastered yet. "But you were right. I've been thinking a lot about it, and I do have some things I need to work on." I sighed. "Basically, what it comes down to is just believing that I deserve better than what I accept."

Beth raised her eyebrows, impressed. "That's definitely a better way of phrasing it, huh?"

As if on cue, Andy walked into the room clutching a beer in his left hand. He sauntered over to us, sliding his right arm around my waist.

"Why are you ladies hiding in here?" he asked, flashing me a lopsided smile.

"Champagne refill," I said. "You?"

"Beer refill." He reached into the fridge and removed a new beer, then tossed the empty bottle into the trash before wandering back into the living room.

Reading Beth's suspicious expression, I knew what she was going to say before she even opened her mouth.

"What about him?" she asked, nodding in Andy's direction. "He seems nice. And he's definitely into you."

"He is," I agreed, shaking my head sadly. "But he's not it."

"How do you know?"

I paused, considering.

"I don't know," I admitted. "But I'll know when I find it."

The next chapter in *My Kick-Ass Life* delved into the art of meditation itself. The previous chapters thus far had focused on identifying your goals and believing you would achieve them, but this chapter gave an actual step-by-step process of how to meditate, how to improve your technique, and what to expect in the long run. Basically, the idea was to set an intention for your practice (i.e.

a question you needed answered, a decision you had to make, etc.) and then sit quietly and clear your mind of all thoughts, allowing your inner voice to guide you in the right direction. It sounded easy, but when I sat down and put it to work, it was much harder than I'd anticipated.

I lit a red candle and kept my gaze fixated on it, trying to focus on my breath, as the book suggested. I asked myself whether or not I should accept Sphinx's offer and move back to California, and sat still, waiting for an answer. Every logical part of my brain told me it was the right decision, but there was something deep inside me that just couldn't pull the trigger. Was it fear of change? Was I scared to leave my friends and family behind? Or was my gut telling me that I belonged here? Because if that was the case, it sure as hell didn't feel like it.

After a few minutes, I figured out why it was called a "meditation practice." This shit was hard. Every time my mind would finally free up, another thought would swoop in and take its place. One second I was focusing on life decisions, and next thing I knew, I was thinking about lasagna recipes. Then I'd catch myself and start over again.

Just as I was finally slipping into the zone, my phone buzzed, throwing my focus off again. I tried to ignore it, but then found my mind wondering who the text message was from, what they wanted, if it was important. Eventually, I gave in and grabbed it.

Oh, God. It was from my mother. There were few things in life I hated more than texting with my mother. She texted like a foreigner. It usually took six back-and-forth messages before I could even figure out what she was saying. And the worst part was, ever since texting had become popular, it was all she wanted to do. She never called anymore. It would've taken half the time to pick up the phone and explain something to me than it would for me to figure it out via short cryptic messages.

Our text conversation went as follows:

Mom: Renters coming June. Need house May.

Me: Huh?

Mom: Rent house first week June.

Me: Verbs would really help here, Mom.

Mom: Need clean house May. You need apartment.

Me: Is that a question or a statement?

Mom: Question.

Me: If you're telling me that you need me out of the house by May to clean it for the June renters, then yes, I will have an apartment by then.

Mom: Okay.

I sat back on the sofa, lost in thought. Was this a sign? Was my mother kicking me out and rendering me homeless the final push I needed to take the plunge? It seemed like too bizarre a coincidence not to be.

Before I drove myself crazy with contemplation, I grabbed my phone again and dialed Jasmine's number.

"Tell me again why I should move back to LA," I said as soon as she picked up.

"Tell me why you shouldn't."

I considered. I looked outside at the snow. I couldn't think of anything.

"I thought you'd already made up your mind," Jasmine said. "What is with you, girl?"

"I don't know. I can't explain it. It's such a no-brainer, right?"

"Um, *yeah*. But if you don't give Michelle an answer soon, she's going to think you're not interested and give the job to someone else."

Ouch. Unemployed *and* homeless.

Jasmine sighed loudly on the other end. "Think about it. Worst case, if you hate it here, which you *won't*, you can always move back."

She was right. Enough indecision. There was a reason I wasn't getting any jobs in Boston, and why my mother was kicking me out of their rental house, and why I had a golden offer and corporate luxury apartment waiting for me on the opposite side of the country. Because that's where I was supposed to be.

"Thank you," I said. "That's exactly what I needed to hear."

And before I could chicken out, I dialed Michelle Lawrence's office line. It rang four times before going to voicemail.

"Hi Michelle, it's Justine Sterling," I said. "I just wanted to let you know that I reviewed your offer and I've decided to accept it. Call me when you're free and we can go over the details."

Michelle was elated. She kept me on the phone for a good 30 minutes, going over the upcoming events I'd be attending, the team members I'd working with, the travel agency that would be managing my corporate housing setup, flight arrangements, and car shipment. I tried to play it cool as we chatted, but secretly I felt like a celebrity. Most girls my age lived in a cramped apartment with roommates, and here I was being put up in luxury housing, with an actual company that paid my airfare and shipping expenses.

Then came the part that made it real.

I was scheduled to start work in four weeks.

Because the next gaming conference was fast approaching, Michelle wanted me to start as soon as possible, so we decided a month would be enough time for me to get settled.

My fantasies of soaking in the jacuzzi at my luxury complex came to a screeching halt as soon as I realized how quickly everything was going to change.

A month…. hmm. I did the math in my head. It would take about a week for my car to be delivered, and another week for me to unpack, shop, and get settled in, so that left… two weeks? I only had two weeks to pack, say goodbye, and leave my life behind!

I thought back to when David and I broke up and I decided to move home. Maybe it was because I was fueled by emotion, but at the time I had never felt so alive. I was determined. I was fearless. I had nothing to lose and everything to gain.

I just couldn't figure out why I didn't feel that way now.

"Do you have any questions?" Michelle asked.

"No, I think we've covered everything," I said. "But if I think of anything, I'll let you know."

"Great. We're so excited to have you on board, Justine."

"Thanks, Michelle. I'm really excited too."

One person who was not excited about the big move, however, was Renee.

I'd barely even finished my sentence before Renee broke down sobbing. Then she blamed it on the hormones and said she understood. Then she broke down sobbing again.

Since she was due in less than two weeks, I promised to stay in Boston until after the baby was born. That seemed to cheer her up. We figured out the benefits of me living in California and talked about all the things we could do together. We could take the baby to Disneyland. Dylan could play shows in LA when he was touring. I could stay with them when I visited Boston during the holidays. By the end of our conversation, we'd already worked out a long-distance plan and I hadn't even left yet.

The rest of the week was spent packing, completing new-hire paperwork, coordinating travel plans, and calling my family members to break the news. But as hard as I tried to envision what my new life was going to be like, it just didn't seem real. I pictured myself wrapping up a kick-ass workday over drinks with Jasmine, hitting pool parties on the weekends, biking along the ocean, shopping at the Grove. I felt the snow being replaced with sunshine. I waited for the excitement to come.

Nothing.

And I finally realized why. It wasn't because I was afraid of going it alone this time, it was because all those things had been much more exciting when Renee was with me. Somehow, beaches and parties and shopping without her felt a little… empty.

But it was too late. I'd made my decision. Plus, Renee had a fiancé and a baby on the way. The days of traipsing around Hollywood together were long gone. So, as much as it hurt my heart, I had to move on with my life, too.

Chapter 23

My last week in Boston was fast approaching, and as predicted, Renee wouldn't let me out of her sight. Every day she called with a new excuse for us to get together, invitations she knew I couldn't decline. She needed help picking out a crib. She needed help painting the baby's room. Dylan was working. She was lonely. I tried to explain how much packing I still had left, not to mention the hour drive there and back. Yet every time, I'd somehow find myself in the driver's seat, heading north to Quincy.

Tonight, I was called in for a celebration. After looking at a few more houses, Renee and Dylan had decided to buy the house in south Boston, which I agreed was perfect for them. They had just received their official approval today, at which point I was called and instructed to bring over a large pizza and my dessert of choice.

What I didn't expect was to walk into Renee's apartment and find seven faces staring at me with matching grins.

"Surprise!" Renee greeted, bombarding me with a hug.

I surveyed the room, my eyes floating from person to person: Renee, Dylan, Andy, Beth, Eddie, our friend Kat, and Kat's husband Christos. All staring at me like I was the president.

"This is… for me?" I asked.

"Come on, you didn't think I was going to let you leave without a party, did you?" Renee joked.

"Oo, pizza," Eddie said, grabbing the box from me and setting it down on the table. He removed a piece and set it down on a plate, while also juggling a king-sized Snickers in his other hand.

Andy cocked an eyebrow. "Dude, what is with you? You eat like a twelve-year-old whose parents are on vacation."

Eddie shrugged, his mouth full of pizza.

"Tell me about it," Beth said. "I've gained so much weight since we moved in together. I told him to stop keeping this crap in the house." She turned to face me. "So, were you surprised?"

Before I could answer, Renee had snuck up behind me. "Obviously she was surprised. Because I really hope she wouldn't wear that to her own party." She gave my neon-blue pants and zebra-printed shirt a once-over. Renee loved to give me a hard time about my fashion sense.

"You're just jealous because you have to wear maternity clothes." I jokingly rolled my eyes at her long-sleeved navy dress. Although I had to admit, with the added tan scarf around her neck, she looked pretty trendy for a mom-to-be.

"At least I don't look like I got dressed in the dark," she teased.

"Funny, I seem to remember a time when you had bangs and dressed like a boy."

"I want to see pictures," Dylan chimed in.

"Only after we're married," she sang.

"You guys are so cute!" Kat yelled, barreling into the room. I had met Kat through Renee years ago, a dark-haired little Greek beauty with a huge personality. Her husband, Christos, didn't say much, but he didn't really need to. His looks alone were enough for me.

Kat linked her arm in mine. "So, are you stoked about your new job?" she asked, her face glowing. I tried to match her reaction, but I felt like a big fake.

"I should be," I admitted, frowning. "I think it just hasn't hit me yet."

"Give it time," she said. "When you're laying on the beach while we're all freezing our asses off, that's probably when it'll sink in."

"True." I forced a smile.

God, what was my problem? Why didn't I feel the excitement that everyone else around me was feeling? Why was I desperately clinging onto a life here that I didn't even want?

"What are going to do if you ever bump into your ex and his fiancé?" came the ever-so-subtle Beth's voice behind me.

I hesitated, debating my response. Of course, I'd imagined the scenario a thousand times in my head, a different outcome occurring each time. Sometimes, I pretended I didn't see them. Sometimes, I made small talk with David and watched him squirm. And sometimes, if I was in an extra-bitter mood, I caused a giant scene, exposing David as the cheating slimeball he was. That was my favorite fantasy, of course, but I'd never do that in real life. I was too much of a wuss.

"Oh, I doubt that will happen," Kat interjected, saving me. "LA's a big city." Sensing my discomfort, she reached out and sat me down on the bar stool next to her. "So, when do you leave?"

"I told my boss that I'm going to stay until after Renee has the baby," I said. "So I'm waiting until then to confirm with the travel agency."

"Oh, speaking of..." Kat grabbed Renee and pulled her over. "Did you know they bought a house?"

"Justine helped me pick it out, actually," Renee said.

"I'm so happy for you guys!" Kat flailed her arms in the air. "You *need* to have a housewarming party."

"We will," Renee said. "Once we're settled in and the weather's a little warmer. I was thinking of getting a little tiki bar for the backyard."

As I listened to Renee and Kat's enthusiasm over their upcoming plans, all I could think about was the fact that these plans didn't include me. I was supposed to be moving forward with my life, but instead I was focusing on all the things I was leaving behind. Here I was, surrounded by a room full of friends, and I had never felt so alone in my life.

Noticing my reaction, Kat shot me a concerned look. "Justine, is everything okay?"

I tried my hardest to hide my disappointment, as I didn't want to be a downer after Renee had organized tonight on my behalf.

"I'm fine," I lied. "I think I…" I looked down just as I felt a splash of water hit the floor. "I think I… just spilled my drink."

Kat's gaze followed mine, then Renee's. "Um, I don't think…" Kat began.

"Oh my God." Renee's jaw dropped, her eyes searching for Dylan. He looked up at her from the other end of the kitchen.

"Was is it?" he asked.

"Dylan," she said, staring down at her dress in shock. "I think my water just broke."

As it turned out, Renee's maternal intuition had a few crossed wires.

Her name was Sierra Cavallari. She was seven pounds, eight ounces, with a little upturned nose, sandy-blonde hair and bright-red cheeks. Even thought her tiny face was right in front of me, it was still a miracle to me that she was real. Renee was a mother. Renee, the girl who had been by my side through everything – teenage concerts, spring-break trips, college parties, girls' weekends in Vegas. Those days were gone. From this point forward, our lives would be forever changed.

When I'd arrived at the hospital that morning, Renee's parents, Dylan's mother, and Beth were already spread across her room, their gazes all frozen on the new arrival. I watched as Dylan's mother scooped Sierra into her petite hands, staring in amazement at her first grandchild. Renee had mentioned that Dylan's father passed away years ago, and I wondered if Mrs. Cavallari was thinking of him right now, if she was remembering the day Dylan was born. If she missed him.

Just then, Kat burst into the room, instantly halting the sentimental family ambiance.

"Look at her!" she screamed, racing toward Sierra. "She

is *beautiful*." She turned to Renee with a skeptical expression. "Mother's intuition my ass."

"I know. I'm never going to hear the end of it." Renee's tired eyes crinkled at the corners, like she wanted to smile but didn't have the energy.

"What's her name?" Kat asked.

"Sierra," Dylan answered proudly.

"Sierra," Kat repeated, lowering her face to meet Sierra's. "Well, Sierra, I hope your mom knows that she'd better call me any time she needs a babysitter."

"Me too," Beth said.

"Me three," Renee's dad joked.

"Well, I don't think you'll have any problems finding a babysitter," Mrs. Cavallari said. Then she leaned down next to Renee and whispered, "But I want first dibs."

I tried to laugh along with everyone until I realized that I was the only one who couldn't volunteer to babysit. In fact, since I was starting a new job and had to accrue vacation time, Sierra would probably be close to a year old before I'd see her again.

"Oh, before I forget…" Renee's mom reached out and handed her a small gift bag. "Just something small that I picked up."

Renee reached into the bag, removing a small white onesie that displayed the phrase *Home is where the heart is* in pink letters across the front.

"Pink?" Renee stared at her accusingly. "Did you know something I didn't?"

"I got one in each color, just in case." Mrs. Evans winked at her.

Dylan took the onesie from her grasp and set it on a table that held all the miscellaneous cards, flowers, and gifts that everyone had brought. But for some reason, I couldn't take my eyes off it.

Home is where the heart is.

That was it. The uncertainty I was experiencing, the reason for my indecision. Home wasn't where a job awaited, or warmer weather, or a more exciting nightlife. LA had felt like home because

I had experienced it with two people I'd loved more than anyone. Regardless whether David had turned out to be a mistake, I had loved him and I had learned from him. And now, I had learned something else.

Boston, with its abundance of snow and apparent lack of jobs, was my home. Because everyone and everything I now loved was here.

"I'm going to go," I spit out, looking toward the door anxiously. I felt a sudden surge of urgency. I had a lot to think about. And very little time.

Everyone in the room turned to me with a look of surprise, except Renee. She knew better.

"Okay," she said calmly. "But actually, before you do, there was something I wanted to ask you." She looked around the room. "Will you guys give Justine and me a minute alone?"

Renee's dad was the first one up and out of his seat. Everyone else followed until the door was closed and we were alone.

I relocated to the chair closest to Renee, looking over at Sierra, who was now asleep in her tiny hospital crib. It was funny to me that, even though I'd only known her for a few hours, I couldn't imagine not being a part of her life.

"I didn't want to ask you this in front of Beth or Kat," Renee began. "But I'd love it if you'd be Sierra's godmother."

"Of course." I said, surprised. That wasn't the question I'd been expecting at all. "But… do you really want me to be her godmother? I mean, what if I'm not living here…?"

"Doesn't matter." She shooed me with her hand. "I wouldn't want anyone else."

I took a deep breath. This was it. Now or never. Because speaking it aloud made it real.

"I'm not going," I blurted out.

"I know."

"I've been trying to figure it out this whole time, and…" I stopped speaking, tilting my head to the side. "Wait, you what?"

Renee smiled knowingly. "You're not going to California. I knew you wouldn't."

My eyebrows creased together. "How did you know before I did?"

"Because I know you. And I could tell. You wanted to, and it makes sense to, but you didn't feel right about it."

"Exactly."

"Justine, there are two types of people in the world – people who do what they're supposed to do, and people who do what they want to do. On paper, moving to LA would be the right decision. But what feels right to you may not be what's deemed 'right' by society. And you're not the type of person who does what's expected of you. A million people can tell you it's the right decision, but if you don't feel that way, you're not going to do it."

I was silent for a moment, as a thought occurred to me. "So, if you knew I wasn't going to LA, then why'd you throw me a party?"

Renee shrugged nonchalantly. "You know me. I'll use any excuse to throw a party."

Chapter 24

I was dreading the call to Michelle so much that I pushed it off for two whole days until I could figure out what I was going to say. I made up a thousand stories – family illnesses, competing job offers, anonymous personal reasons – but then, as always, I realized it was much easier to tell the truth.

Fortunately, after delivering a genuine explanation and apology, Michelle said she completely understood. No travel expenses had been paid yet, so the only thing she'd really lost was time to find a replacement.

I'd been worried that, after withdrawing my candidacy, I'd immediately regret the decision and want to beg for my job back, but it would be too late. Instead, the opposite occurred. The weight I'd been carrying around with me finally lifted, and I knew in my heart I'd made the right decision.

Now if only I could muster up enough courage to break the news to Jasmine…

I decided that call could wait.

Instead, I curled up for the remainder of the night with my new friend, *My Kick-Ass Life*. Considering I was still unemployed, single, and borderline homeless, I was far from leading a kick-ass life. But it was coming. I couldn't explain why, but I was certain it was.

There was an alarm. A deafening, repeating alarm. It shook the walls of the school, echoed through the hallways. Students filed through the classroom doors, making their way toward the exit sign.

David was there. With her. I watched her long mane of blonde hair sway back and forth, her smooth, toned arm intertwined with his. They didn't see me, so I stayed behind, merging with the crowd to blend in.

The alarm grew louder as we approached the exit and my head began to throb. What was David doing at UCLA? Where was the exit? And why was the ringing so loud?

I jumped out of bed, my half-opened eyes scanning the room. My walls, my nightstand, my bed. I was home. I breathed a short sigh of relief, then immediately jumped as I realized the alarm was still ringing.

My phone. Where was my phone? And who was calling me this early?

I reached out and grabbed my cell from the bedside table. It was a number I didn't recognize.

"Hello?" I answered.

"Hello, is this Justine Sterling?"

"Yes it is."

"Hi Justine, my name is Rebecca Falkner. I'm calling from Z-Candy."

Z-Candy… how did I know that name? Why did that sound so familiar?

"Hi Rebecca," I said politely, attempting to pretend I knew who she was.

"You had applied for our online marketing-assistant position," she explained. "I apologize for the delay, but one of our recruiters was on maternity leave, so it's taken us a while to review all the résumés."

Oh. My. God. Oh my God! It was the fashion company! The call I had been waiting for! My dream job!

I looked over at the clock and realized it was almost ten. I cleared my throat and tried to sound more like a functioning member of society and less like an unemployed loser who was still sleeping at ten in the morning.

"Hi Rebecca!" I said. "I'm so happy you called!"

Calm down, Justine, I thought to myself. Don't sound desperate.

Rebecca laughed on the other end. "It's funny how much happier people are to hear from you once they realize you're calling them about a job."

I faked a loud laugh. "Yeah, they're probably happy you're not a… bill collector or something."

Oh, God. Lame joke. Lame. Lame. Lame. The interview was already a mess and I hadn't even set foot in the door yet.

Luckily, for some asinine reason, Rebecca seemed to enjoy my attempted humor. "Right? I can't tell you how many times people have almost hung up on me until I told them who I was."

"Oh, I bet," I said cheesily, like I had any fucking clue about recruiting whatsoever.

"Well, anyway," she continued. "We've received a lot of applicants for this position, but we really liked your résumé. We're looking for a pretty unique skill set, because most candidates either have the marketing experience or the photography experience, but I was so excited to see that you have both!"

If I hadn't been half-asleep, I may have keeled over in shock.

I tried to think of something convincing to say, something that would make Rebecca fall in love with me instantly and offer me the position on the spot. Then I thought back to my conversation with Michelle – all the stupid stories I had concocted to win her sympathy – and the inevitable winning outcome.

Honesty.

"Rebecca," I began, mustering up all the confidence I could in a half-conscious state. "Photography has always been a huge passion of mine. And online marketing is sort of something I fell into when I was in college, but frankly, I'm glad because I'm really good at it. So, to combine both of those things would be a dream job for me."

"That's great to hear!" Rebecca's energy level was too much to handle before my morning coffee. "I know this is kind of short notice, but we had an unexpected opening pop up this afternoon. Would you be able to come in for an interview?"

"Today?" I choked.

"Yes, we had a one o'clock cancellation, so the team is free to meet with you if you think you can make it. Your résumé says you're in the Cape Cod area?"

"Temporarily," I added. "I'm in the process of moving closer to the city."

As soon as I find a job," I thought.

"But if I leave within the hour, I can be there by one," I said.

"Great! I'm going to send you an email now with directions to our office and parking instructions. My contact information will be in the email as well, so call me if you have any problems. We look forward to meeting you!"

"You too! See you soon."

I hung up the phone and jumped around my room. It happened! I had an interview! For my dream job! This was unreal!

The only problem was, I had less than an hour to print extra copies of my résumé, print the interview instructions, figure out where I was going, and get ready.

And, more importantly, what the hell was I going to wear?

I decided on black pants, a black, fitted jacket, a white blouse, and black-suede ankle boots. Bland yet safe, considering I had no idea what the dress code was like.

Naturally, my printer had chosen today, of all days, to be difficult. Which meant that, by the time I had successfully printed copies of my résumé, I didn't have time to shower or do my hair. Which meant that my makeup was applied in the car and the tornado on top of my head looked like a bird's nest.

In short, I was a mess.

The Z-Candy office, however, was anything but. It was everything I had imagined. Artsy, decorative, hip. The lobby was lined with a pink-and-orange sectional sofa, a giant swirly backdrop, and mismatched glass tables on each corner. I sat in the seat closest to the window so I could gaze out at the view of the city.

I had arrived with about 15 minutes to spare, so I sifted though my smart phone, browsing the company history, as I'd always been told to do pre-interview. I learned that Z-Candy had been in business for nine years, had satellite offices in New York and Los Angeles, and were voted one of the top ten best places to work three years in a row by the Boston Globe. I was just about to research how many employees there were when a tall blonde with spiral curls entered the lobby, clutching a tablet in her left hand.

"Justine?" she asked, extending her right hand. "I'm Rebecca Falkner."

I quickly shoved my phone in my purse and stood up to shake her hand. "Great to meet you."

Rebecca led me down a long, white hallway, chatting endlessly about what a crazy morning it'd been and how glad she was that I could make it. I nodded attentively, but only half of me was listening. The other half was focused on Rebecca's outfit – a long-sleeved, fitted coral shirt, teal skinny pants, a matching chunky teal necklace, and purple lace-up ankle boots. It was easy to see why she worked for a fashion company, although Renee would've cringed at her outfit. She looked straight out of an eighties music video. I looked down at my boring black-and-white ensemble, kicking myself for not wearing something a little trendier. It was a fashion company, after all. I should've known better.

But hell, if I did get the job, I'd fit right in. No one would look twice at a zebra shirt/blue pants pairing.

Rebecca sat me down in one of the coolest conference rooms I'd ever seen. Granted, I hadn't seen many since I was a fairly recent college grad, but still. The walls were made of complete glass, so everyone who passed by could see in. Pendant lamps fell from the ceiling in a variety of shapes, lime-green swivel chairs surrounded a giant multi-colored table that looked like it was made of Lego. The room was adjacent to the kitchen, which was stocked with coffee, snacks, and high, pub-style tables. It looked like a restaurant.

Rebecca left the room for a few minutes, returning with three women, who were all dressed similarly to her. I stared at the assortment of colors, stripes, belts, high-waisted pants, chunky heels, flashy jewelry, and couldn't help but feel slightly intimidated. I forced myself to concentrate as each woman introduced herself, remembering that, if I wanted my kick-ass life to start now, I had to ace this interview.

It was clear right off the bat that the woman who introduced herself as Donna Capone was the boss in charge. She appeared slightly older than the other two girls, with a short, brown pixie cut and a no-nonsense demeanor. I smiled politely at Ellie, a petite Asian in a blue dress, and Nora, a tall redhead with guitar-pick earrings, then redirected my attention to Donna as they sat down across from me.

"So, Justine," Donna began, looking down at a copy of my résumé that she'd brought. Dammit. I didn't need to print the extras after all. "Tell us about yourself."

"Well…" I looked back and forth between the three women, trying to come up with something intelligent to say. Or witty. Or… something.

Honesty, I reminded myself. Act normal. Be yourself.

"Well, after meeting all of you, I'm really wishing I hadn't chosen an outfit that makes me look like a school teacher," I blurted out.

The room erupted in laughter. I breathed a sigh of relief.

"It's okay." Donna winked at me. "It's an interview. Better to be safe than sorry."

"Yeah, that's sort of why I picked it out." I blushed. "But seriously, you all look great. And this office is gorgeous."

Donna smiled. "So I take it you have a strong interest in fashion?"

"You could say that," I replied casually. "I've only been waiting for your call for…" I looked down at my pretend watch. "About two months now?"

More laughter.

So far so good.

"Yes, I'm sorry about that," Donna said. "We had a bit of a delay since our senior recruiter went on maternity leave. But luckily you didn't accept any other offers in the interim." Donna pursed her lips together. "Speaking of, do you have any other offers right now? Or are you interviewing elsewhere?"

I considered. I didn't want to sound like a total loser and tell them I had about as much going on in my professional life as I did my love life, but I also wanted them to know how serious I was about this job.

"Well, I was recently offered a position in Los Angeles as an event manager, but after weighing my options, I decided that relocation isn't a good choice for me at this time."

Donna looked intrigued. "Why is that?"

"To be honest, I almost accepted it, because it was a really great offer," I admitted. "But my goddaughter was born yesterday." I paused, smiling. "I took one look at her and knew I wasn't going anywhere."

All three women sighed in unison, looking at each other with soft, nostalgic eyes. I stifled a laugh. All it took was the mention of a baby to win the attention of every female in the room.

"I have two daughters myself," Donna said. "So I completely understand." Her gaze lowered to my résumé, skimming the lines. "Okay, tell us about your online marketing experience at Sphinx. More specifically, I'd like to know what your day-to-day responsibilities were, the social-media outlets you used to promote the business, and any campaigns you participated in."

For the next few minutes, we discussed my position at Sphinx

– how it began as an internship and transitioned into a full-time position, my daily tasks, what I liked and disliked about it. Donna did most of the probing, while Ellie and Nora would occasionally interject with a question or two. Once Donna seemed pleased, she moved on to the next subject.

"As you know, this position requires quite a bit of photography knowledge and experience. You'll need to assist with photographing our new clothing lines, so you need to know about lighting, angles, and have a natural artistic eye. Part of your job is going to be marketing our organization digitally, so you'll need to select the best photos to go on our website and social-media pages, something that will make people want to click on the link and purchase our products." Her eyes burned into mine, like she was about to stress a crucial point. "We don't want to hire a random, part-time freelance photographer. We want someone who knows our products, understands our products, and can capture our products in a way that will really market them."

I nodded.

"Your résumé says you have extensive experience with Photoshop?"

I nodded again.

"What type of camera do you use?"

"The Canon 5D. The image quality is incredible, so it requires much less editing."

Donna grinned. "I'm absolutely clueless when it comes to cameras."

Oh. Well then.

"But," she continued, raising an eyebrow. "I can tell you're not."

My cheeks flushed as I lowered my gaze to the table. Compliments always made me feel shy.

"This is the link to your portfolio?" Donna asked, pointing to my résumé.

"Yes."

She gestured to her tablet. "Do you mind if I pull it up?"

"Not at all."

For the next few minutes, we scrolled through all of my best work – going as far back as high-school and college projects, and ending with Electric Wreck's album cover.

"These are very nice," Donna said when she was finished, setting down her tablet. She looked from Nora to Ellie. "Do you girls have any final questions for Justine?"

Ellie raised her head, tossing me an inquisitive look. "Just one," she said. "Why photography? What is it that you love about it?"

Hmm. That was a hard one. Not because I couldn't think of a reason why I loved it, but because there were so many reasons. It was tough to choose just one.

"Well," I began. "There are a lot of things I love about it, but I think what it comes down to is the sincerity of it."

All three women inched forward in their seats, waiting for me to continue.

"Life moves really quickly," I explained. "Especially in a world where we're so bound to technology. It's easy to miss things, to get distracted by your computer, your phone, your TV. But with photography, you're able to capture moments that you'll never get back. And once you've caught those moments, you have them forever. There's something so beautiful and real about that."

Donna nodded, looking pleased. "Thank you Justine," she said, standing up to shake my hand. "We'll be in touch."

Chapter 25

I felt so good after my interview that I decided to treat myself to an afternoon latte. I stepped out of the Z-candy office and crossed the street to the nearest Starbucks, ducking my face to shield it from the February cold.

Once I was safely inside the warm coffee shop, I ordered a gingerbread latte with whipped cream, then sat down at a table as I waited, reflecting on the past hour. I couldn't believe what had just transpired. Never in my life had I been so honest in front of a room of complete strangers, and it felt great. Even if I didn't land this job, I would know in my heart that I had given it my everything.

The barista called my name, and I stood up and grabbed my coffee, preparing to face the wind chill as I walked to my car. The only problem was that once I was outside, I couldn't remember which direction the parking garage was in. The Z-Candy office was located in a highly commercial area, with parking structures on every corner that looked virtually identical to each other. I started to head north of the building, then turned to face the opposite direction.

Was the structure on the right side of the building? Or the left? I reached into my purse and removed the directions that Rebecca had emailed to me earlier that morning.

Ah, of course. It was *behind* the building.

I crossed the street and began walking towards the rear entrance of the Z-Candy office. But as I looked around, that didn't seem right either. Although, there was something vaguely familiar about the neighborhood. The buildings… the restaurants… it was almost as if I had been here before…

"Justine?"

You had to be kidding.

I blinked several times, focusing on the figure walking toward me.

"Walter?" My jaw dropped. "What are you doing…?"

Wait a second… That was it! This was where Walter's office was! Now it made sense.

"Hey, I work here," he said in a jokingly defensive tone. "I think I should be asking you that question."

"Well, as a matter of fact, I had a job interview." I smiled smugly.

"Look at you, moving up in the world." He grabbed my hand and spun me around in a circle. "Think it went well?"

"I do." My eyes narrowed. "Wait… what are you doing in town? I thought you went back to New York."

"I did, for a few weeks," he explained. "But actually, I just moved here."

"Wow, that's great," I said. "What made your girlfriend change her mind?"

Walter forced an uncomfortable laugh, his eyes faltering to the ground. "Well, she didn't actually," he admitted. "We broke up."

"Oh, I'm sorry," I said, thinking about how Renee was going to have a field day when I broke the news that Walter was single. "Are you okay?"

"Yeah, you know, it was for the best. She's a great person, but my goals are important to me. And if I want to branch out in real estate, part of that requires traveling and sometimes relocating, which wasn't something she was very supportive of." He sighed. "I tried to make it work, but ultimately, when you feel as though someone's holding you back from something, you begin to resent them."

"Yeah, I understand," I said. "Well, if I get the job, maybe we can grab lunch sometime."

Shit. That sounded way too much like I was asking him on a date.

"You know, since our offices are right near each other," I added quickly.

"Yeah, of course," he said. "And I assume if they hire you, we'll have some apartment- hunting to do."

I grinned. "You know it."

He smiled back, brushing my arm with his as he turned to walk away. "Well, in that case, I hope you get the job."

"What do you mean he didn't ask you out?"

I sighed on the other end of the phone. "Renee, the guy just got out of a relationship."

"Whatever." I could hear her chewing on something crunchy. It sounded like chips. "I should threaten to switch real-estate agents unless he takes you out."

"Don't you dare."

"I won't. But I want to." A pause. More chewing. "God, I cannot *believe* he didn't ask you out!"

"I can. You should've seen me. I looked like amplified death."

"I seriously doubt that." Another pause. "So how was the interview anyway?"

I pouted, looking at the clock. "I thought it went really well. But it's been almost two days and… nothing."

"That's not that long."

"Feels like it."

"Well, you know the golden rule – a watched phone never rings."

"I guess that explains why David never called me while I was sleeping with my cell surgically implanted into my hand."

"Exactly. Men can smell desperation a mile away. Or 3,000."

I sat down at my kitchen table, assessing my options. "So, what should I do?"

"Well for one, get out of your fucking house. Go do something. Take your mind off it."

"Like what? Go shopping with all the money I don't have?"

"I don't know. Go for a walk. Something."

"In 15-degree weather?"

"You can come over here. Sierra's sleeping and Dylan's about to head to Great Scott for a sound-check."

"You know, that's not a bad idea." I looked at the clock again. It was a little after four. "I'll be there by six."

As soon as I hung up the phone and set it down, it started ringing. I grabbed it, thinking it was going to be Renee again, but jumped when I saw it was an unfamiliar number.

"Hello?" I answered.

"Justine?" It was a woman's voice. My heart leaped.

"Yes?"

"It's Rebecca Falkner from Z-Candy."

I squeezed my eyes shut. Please, please, please. Let this be it.

"Hi Rebecca," I said carefully. I didn't want to get excited just yet, but I could feel a tingling sensation spreading throughout my entire body before I even knew what she was going to say.

"I have great news," she continued. "The team here loved you and thought your experience was exactly what we're looking for." I could hear her smiling through the phone. "So… we'd like to officially offer you our online marketing-assistant position."

I was ecstatic. It was as if I could finally move forward with my life, like someone had pressed the un-pause button and I could live again. I could move to the city, meet new people, experience new things. I could become a whole new person.

But it didn't stop there.

The job was only the first step. I still had a lot of things to work on before my life was where I wanted it to be – my confidence,

194

being a better friend, letting the right people into my heart. It was a lot, but my new position was a stepping stone. The first stone that would lead to many great things.

Because I was trying to incorporate healthy habits into my daily routine, I spent the entire morning meditating. Surprisingly, the more I practiced, the better I got. I really was beginning to notice a difference in my life. My head felt clearer, like I finally had clarity on what I wanted in life, and how to get there.

Feeling satisfied, I stood up and grabbed my laptop, then sat down at the kitchen table, preparing to send Rebecca my references. The only problem was that I was planning on using Jasmine as one of my references, and I still hadn't told her that I was staying in Boston. I knew she'd understand, but part of me felt bad after all the trouble she went through to get me the job at Sphinx.

Just as I was mustering up the courage to make the call, I heard the sound of my ringtone, but it sounded a million miles away. I wandered from room to room, following the noise, until I reached the bedroom and found it lying on top of my comforter. I quickly grabbed it.

"Hello?" I answered.

"Well, you sound a lot better than the last time I called," said a familiar voice.

I looked down at the unknown number on the screen. "Huh?"

"Or, at least," he continued, "you don't sound like you're waiting for that guy to call anymore."

I sat down on the edge of the bed, swinging my legs in the air. "Walter?"

"Let me guess," he said. "I'm going to assume by your tone of voice that we're going to be apartment-hunting very soon."

I grinned. "We are," I said. "They offered me the job yesterday."

"Congratulations," he said. "That great because… I have something to tell you."

I sat up straight, intrigued. "What's that?"

"Well, the reason I'm calling is because I think I've found the perfect place for you."

"Really? How do you know?"

"Based on the other apartment you liked, I think I know your taste." I could picture him shrugging nonchalantly on the other end. "It's my job to know these things."

"Good point."

"When do you start your new job?"

"I don't know yet. They have to check my references, so I won't know until next week."

"Okay. Are you free next Friday? Maybe we could meet at my office and go look at this place?"

"Friday works for me."

"Great. If you want to meet at my office around four, I can drive."

"Sounds good."

"I was also wondering if… maybe you'd want to grab dinner after?" he asked." If you're not busy. I thought maybe we could celebrate your new job."

"Sure. That sounds like fun."

"Okay," he said, sounding relieved. "I'll see you then."

With my new job and future apartment lined up, there was one last task I needed to complete. To call Jasmine and break the news that I was staying in Boston.

Normally, my stomach would've been in knots as I waited for her to answer, since I hated disappointing people. Not today, though. Today, I was excited to have someone to share my news with.

"Hey, girl," she answered. From the noise in the background, I could tell she was driving. "How's things?"

"Things are great."

"Good. When are you getting your ass out here?"

"Well, about that…" I fidgeted with my hair nervously. "I have something I need to tell you."

She exhaled loudly. "I knew it. You're not coming are you?"

I launched into the entire story – from my initial doubts to meeting Sierra to getting the offer at Z-Candy. When I finished, I sat in silence and waited, hoping she wasn't too upset.

"Well," she finally said. "As much as I'm going to miss having you here, I'm really happy for you. I know how much you wanted that job."

I breathed a heavy sigh of relief. "Thank you. I was hoping you'd say that. To be honest, I'm surprised you hadn't heard by now. I already told Michelle."

"I've been at a conference all week. Haven't really been in the office. You know how it goes."

"Yeah." I paused. "And... there's something else too."

"What's that?"

"Are you still driving?" I asked her.

"I just got home. Why?"

"Go to your computer and look up Walter Keller real estate."

I waited as she typed and clicked.

"Ohh," she mumbled. "*Ohhh.* Damn. Who the *hell* is that?"

"That's the agent who's getting me an apartment."

"With looks like his, that better not be all you're getting." She continued to make perverted noises as she clicked away.

"Well, he did ask me to grab dinner with him Friday night after we look at the apartment, but I don't think a date. He..."

"It's a date."

"But he just got out of a relationship, so..."

"It's a date."

"What if it's just a business thing? We had lunch the last time we looked at apartments."

"Justine, lunch and dinner are two different things. A man does not ask a woman to dinner unless he's at least mildly interested."

I paused, considering. "Really? You think?"

I could hear her chuckling on the other end. "For your sake... I sure as hell hope so."

Chapter 26

For my night out with Walter, I wanted to wear something semi-casual (as apartment-hunting seemed like a jeans-and-sweater type of activity), but still dressy enough to wear to dinner. I decided on black skinny jeans with gray knee boots, a dark-purple sweater, and a multi-colored scarf around my neck. I added a few subtle curls in my long, brown hair, applied a layer of red lipstick, and accessorized with lots of jewelry.

Beauty Tip #1: When in doubt, jewelry and makeup can dress up any outfit.

The drive to Walter's office went by amazingly fast, probably because I checked my reflection in the visor mirror about 65 times while overanalyzing Jasmine's words and hoping Walter didn't think this was an actual date. The last thing I needed was a gorgeous guy on the rebound toying with my already broken heart.

After parking my car in the back lot per his instructions, I stole one last glance at myself as I walked towards his office, smoothing my hair in the glass-door reflection. My curls were still intact, my lipstick fresh, my scarf adding a touch of class. Although I did wish my skin had a bit more color. I had applied a layer of blush to my cheeks, but the pale skin still peeked out from underneath.

I strolled through the door and spotted Walter emerging from his office in a white button-up and dark-gray dress pants.

"Hey," I greeted, waving to him.

"Hey. Good to see you." He leaned in and gave me hug, then pulled back and studied me for a brief moment. "You ready to go?"

I nodded and followed him as he grabbed a long, black coat from the wall rack and led me to his car.

We made small talk as he drove south on route 93. I told him the details about my new position at Z-Candy, Renee's new baby, my declined opportunity in LA. He filled me in on his move from New York, how he was starting to get familiar with the Boston area, that he sometimes missed home.

He exited the freeway in south Boston, and after a few turns I began to get a feeling of déjà vu. I looked at him curiously.

"Is this the way we came when we looked at Renee's house?" I asked.

He shook his head but said nothing. He looked like he was holding back a smirk, like he knew something I didn't.

After a few minutes, he pulled the car into a parking lot, and I recognized the building immediately.

"Wait a second…" I said, glancing up. "This is the building… of the apartment I loved!"

Walter grinned, throwing the car into park. "Very good."

I thought for a minute. "So they have another vacant apartment?"

He nodded.

"Is it similar to the one we looked at before?"

"You'll see," he said, climbing out of the car. I got out and followed him into the building.

We rode the elevator up to the third floor and got off, stopping at the second door on the right. Walter snuck a peek at me over his shoulder as he unlocked the door, his eyes turned up at the corners.

As soon as I stepped through the door and looked around, I burst out laughing. Now I understood. It didn't just look like the same apartment, it *was* the same apartment. Only this time, the walls had been painted a light beige, and the kitchen had been upgraded with cherry wood cabinets.

"Very funny," I said. "So what happened? The renters backed out?"

"They did. Turns out the couple that was going to move in broke up."

"Lucky for me."

"And me. They would've been nightmare clients."

"Why's that?"

"Turns out, the guy was cheating on his girlfriend." He held his hands up in defense. "I didn't ask or anything, but his girlfriend felt the need to tell me the entire story. I think she just wanted someone to vent to." He shrugged. "So if that was going on, I imagine they probably would've wanted out of their lease sooner or later."

I nodded in agreement. "You must see a lot of crazy things working in real estate."

Walter's eyes twinkled, like he was having a private joke with himself. "You have no idea." He started to open his mouth, then stopped. "Why don't we get out of here, and I'll tell you some stories over dinner. Unless… you want to look around a bit more?"

"No, that's okay," I said. "I've seen enough."

"And?"

"And… I love it. Even more than before."

"Okay," he said, linking his arm in mine. "Then I guess we have two things to celebrate tonight."

For dinner, Walter suggested that we leave his car at his place and walk to a nearby restaurant, since he lived in Central Square in Cambridge and there were plenty of local options. I clutched my jacket tight as we set foot into the cold winter night, strolling through the square.

"Do you like tapas?" he asked, gesturing to a yellow-painted restaurant on the next block.

"I do," I said. Renee and I had a favorite tapas restaurant in

LA that we'd frequented, and I loved the variety of sampling different plates.

"Great," he said, fidgeting with his coat. "I know I haven't lived here long, but so far this is my favorite place yet."

I followed him into the restaurant, a quaint little gem with an adorable abundance of quirky knick-knacks. Every lamp, chandelier, painting, and sculpture were mismatched, an artistic assortment that made me wish I'd brought my camera to capture the intricate little details. I'd always loved restaurant ambiance more than the food itself. To me, it was about the experience – cozy atmosphere, fine wine, good conversation.

We sat down at a table in the corner, and for the next hour I forced myself to relax and just have fun. Even if this technically wasn't a date, it was the closest thing to a date I'd experienced since David. I told myself to treat it as a practice run, the first step in getting back out there.

And just as I was starting to get comfortable, I leaned in a little too far, causing my glass of red wine to tip over and explode all over Walter's white button-up shirt.

My jaw dropped in horror as I watched it unfold. It was like a bad movie. Walter jumping up from the table, waitresses rushing over with napkins, my cheeks flushing the same shade as the wine.

Fortunately, after our table was cleaned up and I apologized a million times, things started to go uphill. Walter and I snacked on hummus and pita bread, grilled zucchini with feta, kale salad with pear and pecans. I wasn't much of a meat-eater but I splurged and tried the crispy prosciutto with burrata cheese and Brussels sprouts with bacon. My mouth was in heaven. Just when I thought it couldn't get any better, another plate would come and spark my tastebuds all over again.

Our waitress stopped by the table to check on us, and I decided to switch from wine to cocktails, since they had a great drink menu. I ordered the "Berry Fusion", which consisted of muddled strawberries and blueberries with flavored vodka and a splash of soda water. When the waitress walked away, I noticed Walter looking at me funny.

"What?" I asked, hoping I didn't have any food on my face. That would really top off the night.

"You do remember you have to drive tonight, right?" There was a slight condescending tone in his voice. "You might want to ease up on the drinks."

Shit. I felt like a heel. I'd completely forgotten I had left my car back at his office.

Great. Now in addition to being a klutz, I was also an alcoholic.

I lowered my gaze to the floor. "I'll be fine," I mumbled.

Walter's eyes softened. "I'm sorry," he said, hanging his head. "I didn't mean to sound like an asshole. I just... want to make sure you get home okay."

"It's fine," I said in a defensive voice. "It's just been a bad couple of months, and tonight all I wanted was to go out and try to have a good time."

The waitress came over and dropped off my drink, which I proceeded to finish in three sips. Walter looked at me with an amused expression.

"Listen," he began. "I really am sorry. But in all seriousness, you're welcome to come to my place after this. You can stay as long as you'd like, until you're ready to drive home."

"Okay," I agreed, forcing a smile. "Why don't we grab some coffee and dessert, and then I'll see how I feel."

Walter grinned, passing me a dessert menu. "You're in luck," he said. "Because their spicy chocolate churros are to *die* for."

Chapter 27

I awoke the next morning to the smell of bacon. The clanging of pots and pans echoed from the kitchen, along with the faint hum of music. I sat up straight in a bed that was most certainly not mine, looking around the room. On the bedside table next to me was a photo of two guys. I picked it up and recognized Walter as one of them.

Oh, no.

I looked down and breathed a sigh of relief that I was still wearing my clothes.

Okay, I hadn't slept with him. Phew. I sat still for a moment, listening to the sound of Walter cooking, trying to remember what had transpired after dinner. I hadn't drank that much...

Oh. *Now* I remembered. After we'd arrived at his place, Walter cracked open a bottle of wine and offered me his bed for the night so I didn't have to drive home. That explained my lack of memory. I cringed as bits and pieces of the night came back to me – Walter divulging details about his breakup, me reciprocating by telling him about David and his fiancé.

The last thing I remembered was Walter tucking me into his bed and going to sleep on the couch.

I climbed out of bed and tiptoed to the kitchen, sneaking a peek before he noticed me. There he was, bent over the stove in navy gym shorts and a fitted, gray t-shirt that clung to his biceps.

Walter noticed me out of the corner of his eye, spinning around to face me.

"There she is," he said, flipping a stack of bacon onto a plate. I could tell instantly that he was much more at ease than he'd been last night. His eyes seemed like they were smiling at me.

"Hi," I said, stepping shyly into the kitchen. I stood there awkwardly for a second, unsure of where to go. Should I sit down? Stand? Offer to help?

"I know you're not a big a meat-eater," he said, gesturing to the bacon. "But since you indulged last night, I figured…"

"It's fine," I assured him.

"Plus," he said, pointing to another pan that contained a row of French toast. "This was all I had." He shrugged apologetically. "You want some coffee?"

My eyes lit up. There was nothing I loved more than a cup of coffee immediately upon awakening. Apparently my face gave it away because Walter grinned and poured me a cup.

"Cream and sugar are over there." He gestured to the kitchen table. "Help yourself."

I took the mug and sat down at the table, stirring the condiments into my coffee. Walter joined me with two plates of food, placing the butter and syrup in the center of the table.

"You sleep okay?" he asked.

I nodded, slicing my toast into squares. "I did. Thanks for letting me stay here."

"No problem. I had fun." He smiled at me warmly. "Except for the fact that my shirt didn't survive."

I almost choked on my food, which made us both break into laughter.

After we finished, Walter cleared our plates, and I snuck into the bathroom to freshen up. I combed my hair and applied a layer of foundation, mascara, and lip gloss, then grabbed my purse and headed into the living room.

"You ready to go?" Walter asked.

I nodded. "Thanks again for letting me crash here," I said. "And for breakfast."

He leaned in and hugged me, then pulled back slightly, holding me far enough away to stare at my face.

"Listen, I think you're a really cool girl." He stepped back a little more, studying me as he spoke. "And I think we're both in a similar situation and could probably use each other right now. So... what do you say? Friends?"

I smiled, nodding in agreement.

"I'd like that," I said.

I spent the next two weeks enjoying my final days as a free woman. According to Rebecca, that was how much time they needed before I could start, as their background checks typically took over a week to clear. So I filled up my days reading, shopping, and more often than not, on the phone with Walter.

Somehow, over the past two weeks, the two of us had actually become pretty good friends. It started with his phone calls and emails about my new apartment, which turned into visits to his office to fill out paperwork. Which turned into late lunches. Which turned into early happy hours. Next thing I knew, our business calls had transformed into personal calls, and I had one hell of a good-looking new friend.

When I wasn't spending my days talking to Walter, I was either out buying new clothes for work (now that I had a future paycheck lined up and wasn't afraid to splurge), or finishing the final pages of *My Kick-Ass Life*. The last chapter focused on forgiveness and why it was important to forgive people who had wronged you. That one really resonated with me. I think it was because I'd held on to resentment towards David for so long, which was ultimately the reason it had been difficult to move forward.

But David wasn't the only person I'd held animosity towards. And if I was going to give myself a fresh start, I had to cover all

205

bases.

I picked up my phone and dialed Renee's number.

"Hey," I said. "I'm going to be up your way tomorrow and I was wondering if you wanted to grab lunch."

"Sure," she agreed. "Tomorrow's perfect actually because Dylan has the day off, so he can watch Sierra. What are you doing up here?"

"I have to swing by Walter's office and drop off some paperwork for the apartment application."

"Oh. How's that going?"

"They're running a credit check now. I just have to drop off a copy of Z-Candy's offer letter since I don't have a paystub that shows my salary yet, and sign a couple of other things. I should know this week if I'm approved."

"I hope so. If would be awesome if you lived so close."

"I know. I can show you where the apartment is tomorrow. Want me to head to your place around noon?"

"Sure."

I paused, reflecting back on everything I'd learned. My lessons. My fresh start. New beginnings.

"And one other thing," I continued. "I was thinking... maybe you could invite Beth to come with us."

"He likes you," Renee said on the drive back from Walter's office. "He totally likes you."

On the way to lunch, I had picked Renee up and brought her with me to the Keller Realty office, which she had not stopped talked about throughout the entire ride to the restaurant.

"I already told you," I said, rolling my eyes. "We're just friends."

"Friends my ass." She looked at me skeptically. "Did you see the way he looked at you when you walked in? It was like the world had stopped."

"You're really not helping." I pulled into the parking lot of the Italian restaurant where we had agreed to meet Beth and slid into a space.

"Helping what?"

I grabbed my purse from the backseat and stepped out of the car, feeling hopelessly frustrated. It was impossible to explain, but I was really enjoying my friendship with Walter. He made me feel good, and it had been a long time since someone had made me feel that way. The last thing I wanted was to ruin it with expectations.

Beth was already waiting in a booth when we walked in, snacking on a plate of rolls and olive oil. As soon as we sat down, Renee wasted no time filling Beth in on our afternoon.

"You should've seen him," Renee said, grabbing a piece of bread from the basket. "I think it took him a good five minutes before he even noticed I was there."

Beth squinted at me, her little observant eyes analyzing my sour expression. I reminded myself to be nice. It was my idea to invite her, after all.

"So if he's such a catch, then what's the problem?" she asked.

I sighed, resting my chin in my hands. "The problem, as I've explained to Renee, is that I don't want to date him. We both just got out of a relationship, and frankly, I like being friends with him." I looked at each of them defensively. "It's nice to talk to a guy on the phone without worrying about saying something stupid, or to go to lunch with him and not wonder if I'm wearing too much lipstick or the wrong-color shirt." I leaned back in my seat and crossed my arms. "I'm sick of going from guy to guy, trying to impress them. I want to concentrate on myself for a while. Learn how to be alone."

Beth raised her eyebrows in surprise. "Renee, I hate to say it," she said. "But she's right. I don't care how gorgeous this guy is, there's nothing sexier than an independent woman."

I looked at Renee triumphantly.

"You don't need a guy to make you happy," Beth continued. "Especially right now. Give yourself time to get over David. Focus on you."

Before I could reply, my cell phone rang. I glanced down at the caller ID.

"Speak of the devil," I said, lifting the phone to my ear.

"Talking about me, huh?" Walter said on the other end.

"Only bad things."

"Naturally," he joked. "Although, that might change after this conversation is over."

"Oh really? And why is that?"

Renee shot Beth a look that said, *I told you so.*

"Well, let's just say… I may have expedited your apartment approval."

"Really?" My jaw dropped. "That was so fast!"

"Yeah, I forwarded your salary info as soon as you left, and your credit check's already cleared. So you just have to come in and sign the lease and the keys are all yours."

My eyes met Renee's, who was almost as excited as I was. "You got the apartment?" she mouthed.

I nodded, still wide-eyed with surprise.

"Walter, thank you so much," I said. "I'm actually out to lunch right now, so let me call you when I leave."

"You got it. Have fun."

I hung up the phone and clapped my hands in excitement.

"We're going to be neighbors!" Renee yelled. "I'm so excited!"

I couldn't stop beaming, thinking of what was to come. New job, new apartment, new life.

It was all happening.

Chapter 28

I met up with Walter the next day. His office was closed on Sundays, so he agreed to meet me at the apartment and bring the lease agreement and my set of keys. I was so elated I could barely stand it. My own apartment, in the city. I had never lived with anyone except Renee and David, but now I was considering the possibilities. I could decorate the walls any way I wanted, hang my favorite photography pieces, buy bohemian artwork, splurge on expensive furniture. With no one's input to consider but my own.

Walter arrived wearing his Sunday best – worn jeans, a maroon hoodie, and black converse sneakers. He walked to the back entrance of the building, where I was anxiously waiting. When he got close enough, he raised his right hand, dangling a set of keys in front of me.

"I believe these are for you," he said, handing them to me. "The gold one is for the apartment, the silver one is for the laundry room, and the little one is for the mailbox. I'll show you where they are."

Walter led me to a basement full of washers and dryers, briefly showing me how to work the machines, then back up the stairs to the mailroom. Once I had learned my way around the building, we took the elevator up to my new place.

As soon as I opened the door, I immediately noticed a bottle of sparkling cider and two flutes propped on the kitchen counter. I burst out laughing.

"Wow," I said, taking the bottle into my hands. "Do you spoil all your clients with gifts?"

"Only the pretty ones."

"Thank you."

"For the bottle or the compliment?"

I considered. "Both."

"I was going to get you the real thing, but unfortunately, I have to drive tonight," he said.

I popped the bottle open and poured each of us a glass, then handed his glass to him. "So where are you going tonight?"

"I have to head to New York."

"What for?"

He glanced down at his hands. "My ex is moving into a smaller place, so I have to go pick up the rest of my things. I still have a bunch of stuff there."

For a split second, I felt a pang in the pit of my stomach. I reminded myself that we were just friends, and that I had absolutely no reason to be jealous that he was going to see his ex.

"Oh." I nodded nonchalantly, as though I couldn't care less. "Do you guys talk on a regular basis?"

"No," he said in a firm tone. "I think she's a great girl and I'm sure we'll be friends someday, but not right now."

"Too soon," I added.

"Yeah. I think most couples that split need time apart before they can be friends. You need space to let the feelings fade so you can move on. It's hard to do that if they're still in your life." He pointed his index finger at me. "Remember what I told you about breakups. They're painful as hell, but then one day, you wake up, and the sun shines again." He smiled knowingly. "That's when you're ready to be friends."

I was silent for a minute, trying to picture David and me as friends. It was a tough thing to imagine.

Reading my mind, Walter said, "Unless you had a really bad breakup. Then that may not be the best idea."

"My thoughts exactly," I said. "Are you nervous? To see her?"

Walter tapped his thumb against his chin. "To be honest, I'm not looking forward to it. I have no idea how I'm going to feel. But I'm going to see some friends of mine when I'm there too, so that'll be fun. I'll be back tomorrow night." He slid closer to me, his hand resting on the counter. "So, since we're going to be working in the same neighborhood now, maybe we can grab lunch next week."

"Sure. You'll have to show me the area."

"You got it." His light eyes gazed down at me. "I'll call you when I get back in town."

By Friday, I still hadn't heard from Walter. I'd like to say that I was so busy with my new job and moving into my apartment that I hadn't noticed, but that would be a giant lie.

Because, truth be told, I couldn't stop thinking about him.

I was dying to know what had happened in New York. And the more silent my phone was, the more questions arose. Did he see his ex and realize he wasn't over her? Did they decide to get back together? Was that why I hadn't heard from him?

Or maybe, now that everything was finalized with my apartment, he had no reason to call me anymore. Our conversations and get-togethers had always stemmed from something to do with my application. Maybe I was just another real-estate deal. Maybe he was just smooth- talking me to get more business.

No, no. Walter was one of the good ones, I reminded myself. He wouldn't have asked me to lunch if he hadn't meant it.

Then again, he'd also said he'd call me this week. And he hadn't.

Aside from watching my non-ringing phone, my week had mainly consisted of new-hire orientations, training sessions, and furniture-shopping. Each day after work, I headed over to move boxes into my new place, then hit all the local shops. So far, I had ordered a custom-made dark-purple sofa set that would be delivered in two weeks, printed my favorite photography pieces and bought a set of matching frames, and scored a cute kitchen table set from the classified ads.

All in all, it had been a pretty productive week.

By Friday afternoon, my first week of training was complete, so I spent the last few hours in the studio taking test shoots for Z-Candy's new spring line, then decided to head out around five. I was surprised at their schedule flexibility. Most companies had at a strict start/stop time, but Z-Candy's environment was as anti-micromanagement as it got. You could come in and leave whenever you wanted, as long as you got your work done. Between the fashionable crew and the laid-back vibe, I loved it already. I couldn't wait until I was completely trained and could dive headfirst into the work.

On the way home, I stopped at the apartment to drop off a few more boxes. My bed was being delivered tomorrow afternoon, so I could officially move the rest of my things in by the end of the weekend. I'd just have to live without a couch for two more weeks.

I decided to spend the next few hours unpacking and head home once traffic had died down. I began removing the items from each box, starting with the bathroom necessities. I filed my lotions and hair-product bottles in the bathroom cabinet, folded and stacked the towels in the closet, then moved on to the kitchen.

As I emptied my dishes into the kitchen cabinets, my head began to feel like it was swimming underwater. I couldn't help but wonder if Renee had been right. Maybe I had made a mistake by voluntarily placing myself in the friend zone with Walter. What happened someday when the two of us were really to date again? Was Renee's theory true? Did Walter really like me? Or had I made myself completely undateable? And why was I stressing so much about it?

Just as I was lifting my box of wine glasses, my phone rang, causing me to almost drop the entire box. I leaped across the living room, my heart racing at the possibility that it might be Walter.

I reached into my purse, grasping hastily for my phone. But when I saw the name on the ID, my heart began to race even more. Only in a different direction.

You had *got* to be kidding me.

It was the number I had been waiting to appear on my screen for months. The number I'd been dreaming of, begging for. Only now, the only emotion I felt was disappointment.

Funny how things work out sometimes.

I stared at my phone for a minute, debating on whether or not to pick up. Chuckling to myself, I reluctantly pressed the answer button.

"Hi, David," I said into the receiver.

"Hey." His voice was soft and flat, almost as if he had just woken up. "Are you, um… are you busy?"

I glanced around the room at my mess of belongings. "Sort of. Just unpacking. What's up?"

"Oh." I heard a slight lift in his voice. "So you're back here now? For good?"

I had to bite my lip to keep from laughing. It fucking figured. The second I was waiting for someone else to call, David chose that moment to reappear. It was like the universe was playing a big joke on me.

I started to tell him the truth, then stopped, thinking better of it. "Why do you ask?"

He paused, moaning contemplatively. "Well you mentioned that you were thinking of moving back, so I figured…"

"That you'd call to check in?" I rolled my eyes. "And how would your fiancé feel about that?"

He sighed loudly on the other end. "We, um… we broke up."

I grinned wickedly. I couldn't help it. Every bone in my body was doing the karma dance. "Smart girl."

"She dumped me for some actor." His voice was lifeless. He couldn't even conceal the heartache.

"Oh? Anyone I'd know?" I cupped my hand over my mouth. This was too much fun.

"No," he said defensively. "He's like a D-list actor. He hasn't even had any big parts or anything."

"And you would know this because..."

Silence.

"Because... you stalked his IMDB page?" I offered, thinking back to when I was trolling Fiona's modeling portfolio.

Everything really does come full circle, doesn't it?

"It's a shitty feeling, isn't it?" I asked.

More silence.

"Yeah, it is," he finally mumbled. "And I know I deserve it. But that's not why I'm calling. I just..." There was a long pause. "The last time I saw you... I didn't want to leave things like that."

"So, now that you're single, you figured you'd try to make amends."

God, Beth was so right. I thought back to her words, which now felt like a million years ago.

The minute they break up, he's going to do exactly what he did with Renee. He's going to call you and beg for forgiveness, and by then, you're going to be long over him.

I knew that's why he was calling. He was secretly hoping that I was back in town, so he could try and sweet-talk me into coming over. Sweet little naïve Justine to the rescue. Someone to feed his ego. Console his broken heart.

"Listen, David, I'm sorry you're hurting right now," I said. "But I'm not that girl anymore. I'm not going to come running every time you call. And considering the fact that you not only cheated on both Renee and your fiancé, but you also lied to me about your engagement to get me into bed, you're not the person I thought you were either."

"I didn't expect you to want to see me," he said. "I just wanted to tell you that I'm sorry. For everything." He exhaled loudly. "I hope you'll accept my apology."

"I do," I said. And I meant it. I thought back to what I'd read about forgiveness. How it was the only way to move on.

"Really?" There was a trace of hope in his voice. "So do you think…"

"I also took a job offer in Boston," I interjected. "So it looks like I'm staying here."

"Oh." His voice fell. "Well, I'm happy for you."

"Thanks," I said. "Take care of yourself, David."

I hung up the phone and sat down on my kitchen chair, staring blankly at the wall in front of me. Six months ago, I would've leaped in excitement over that call, raced to Logan Airport, and boarded the first plane back to LA.

Now, I felt… nothing.

Sure, there was a little satisfaction in knowing that David was brokenhearted, but mostly I just felt relieved.

I guess the book was right. There was something about forgiveness that was freeing.

Although, I had to admit… every time I thought about David crying over Fiona, I smiled a little on the inside.

Chapter 29

It was after eight when I finished unpacking. So far, the bathroom and kitchen were both stocked, my bookshelf was organized, and some of my clothes were hung up in the closet. I still had a bunch of things left at my parents' house, but so far, I was making pretty good headway.

I sat down at the kitchen table (the only place to sit), and rested my chin in my hands. I wished so badly that my bed was here so I could pass out. I was beyond tired, and an hour's drive back to Cape Cod was the last thing I wanted.

I cradled my cell in my hands, thinking back to my conversation with David. Ironically, instead of calling Renee or Jasmine, the one person I wanted to share the story with was Walter. We'd been discussing our past relationships so much lately that my first instinct was to call him. I knew he'd laugh just as hard as I did.

Screw it, I thought, looking down at my phone. Friends can call each other, right? Wasn't that the whole point of being friends? So you didn't have to play games?

Before I could overanalyze anymore, I dialed his number and pushed the call button.

After four rings, his voicemail picked up. I hung up and set the phone down on the table, my heart heavy with disappointment. There was only one reason I could think of as to why I hadn't heard from him all week, and why he was now ignoring my calls.

I just hoped she realized how lucky she was.

But really, what was I thinking? I could never be just friends with Walter. It was inevitable that one of us would develop feelings (one of us = me), so I guess it was better to cut ties now than to be hurt later.

I stood up, picked up my purse, and headed to the door. Surprisingly, despite the slight sting in my chest, I felt okay. I reminded myself that I was supposed to be focusing on me, and when the timing was right and the right guy came along, I'd be ready.

I just didn't expect him to be standing on the other side of the door when I opened it.

I jumped back in surprise, just as Walter was raising his hand to knock. His eyes crinkled at the corners.

"Well if that ain't good timing, I don't know what is," he said, the little-boy grin emerging.

I stood there speechless for a minute, admiring the cute way his gray-collared shirt was slightly untucked from his navy dress pants. Like he'd had a long day at work and given up on his appearance by the end of it. Before he could say anything else, I moved closer to him, falling into his arms.

"Wow," he said, pulling me in tight. "If I didn't know any better, I'd think you missed me."

"I hadn't heard from you all week," I said, my voice muffled against his chest. "I was starting to think you'd used me for a business deal."

He let out a loud laugh, then lowered himself so our faces were level with each other. "Sorry about that. It's been a crazy week."

I stepped backward into the apartment, and he followed me inside. I shut the door, then spun around to face him. "So you didn't get back with your ex-girlfriend?"

Walter raised his eyebrows in surprise. "What? No. Of course not." Curiosity shimmered across his face. "Why would you think

217

that?"

I shrugged. "I just figured since I hadn't heard from you…"

He looked at me sympathetically. "Not at all. I've just been slammed with work. One of those weeks."

"Oh. What are you doing here, anyway?"

"I was in the building." He gestured in the direction of the hallway. "We're renting out one of the other units on this floor, so I had to stop by and take care of a few things. I just saw that you called, so I figured I'd stop by and see if you were here."

He surveyed the living room, then wandered to the bedroom, peeking inside the closets. "Looks like you're making progress."

"Yeah. My bed's being delivered tomorrow, so I can move the rest of my stuff in this weekend."

I followed him into the kitchen, and we each sat down at the table.

"So," I began hesitantly. "How was your trip?"

He rolled his head in a circle, like he was gauging how much to disclose. He still seemed a little guarded when it came to opening up. "You know, I'm glad I went. I thought it was going to be hard, but truthfully… it was exactly what I needed."

"Closure?" I suggested.

His eyes lit up. "Yeah. Exactly. I guess part of me wondered if I'd done the right thing, if maybe I should've stayed and tried to work it out." He winced. "Like maybe I was being selfish by putting my goals before her, you know?"

I shrugged. It didn't sound all that selfish to me.

"That was how she made me feel anyway." His gaze fell. "But when I saw her this past weekend, I realized I did the right thing. I mean, goals are important to me, but so are relationships. And, if I'm being completely honest, I think if I really loved her, I would've stayed."

"But you didn't," I finished.

He shook his head sadly. "I tried to. And for a while, I thought I did. But I think I was just forcing something that wasn't there because I thought it was the right thing to do. Everything about her was perfect, but something was always missing."

I had seen that happen a lot. People had a tendency to do what they were supposed to do rather than what they wanted to do, so a lot of times, they'd commit to the person who checked off all the boxes. What they didn't realize was that it was the person who didn't check off the boxes that they really fell for. The person who introduced them to new things, forced them to step outside of their comfort zone, pushed them beyond their limits. Inspiration was a crucial element to relationships that was, unfortunately, often overlooked.

"I've been there," I said, thinking back to my ex-boyfriend, Mark Wheeler. He was the best catch a girl could ask for, and I couldn't have been more bored. "But you know what they say. Good on paper, bad in bed."

Walter jerked back, pretending to be offended. "Are you saying I'm bad in bed?"

"Are you saying you're good on paper?"

We both laughed, falling easily into the banter with each other. "Speaking of, I have something funny to tell you," I said. "Guess who just called to see if I moved back to LA?"

"*No.*" Walter's eyes widened.

I nodded excitedly. "And guess whose fiancé just dumped him for an actor?"

He tossed his head back, howling. "So what did you tell him?"

I swallowed, trying to keep a straight face. "I told him to come out to Boston so we can talk about things. He's going to fly out next weekend."

Walter's face darkened. He was silent for a minute, studying my expression. "Really?"

I broke into a grin. "No. Not really." I rolled my eyes at the thought. "God, no."

He reached out and punched my arm playfully, his shoulders heaving with relief. "I was gonna say…" His brow knotted. "So what did you really tell him?"

"That I'm not the same person I was before." I shrugged. "And that he isn't the person I thought he was."

"And how do you feel?"

"Better than I've felt in a long time."

"I'm glad to hear that because…" Walter fell silent, his eyes trained on the wall behind me. "Part of the reason I've been MIA this week is because there was something else I realized when I went to see my ex."

My heart began to race. "What's that?"

He traced his jaw line with his thumb, looking at me warily. "You know, I wasn't going to say anything, given the circumstances, but… I've been thinking a lot about you."

"So you've been MIA because…"

The corners of his lips curved upward. "Because it's hard to be friends with someone you have feelings for."

I broke into a grin. "Yeah. I know the feeling."

Before I had time to process what was happening, Walter was off his chair, pulling me to my feet. He took my hands in his, his expression serious.

"I know we haven't known each other very long, but Justine…" He looked straight into my eyes. "I never felt the way about my ex that I feel about you. And seeing her this weekend confirmed that. I guess I thought that when I saw her, some feelings would still be there, but truthfully, all I could think about this weekend was you."

I stood there, open-mouthed, waiting for him to continue.

"I kept wishing you were with me," he said. "I passed an art gallery and thought about how much you'd love the photography, and how much more fun the trip would be if you were there." His eyes fell to the floor. "I guess that's part of what was missing. My ex and I never really had fun together. But with you it's… different. Everything's more exciting when you're around." He looked me up and down mischievously. "Not to mention, you're pretty damn gorgeous. And any guy who doesn't want to be with

220

you is a complete fool."

I laughed, my cheeks reddening.

"I know the timing isn't great," he admitted. "But I don't know how much longer I can go on pretending that this…" He gestured between the two of us. "Isn't here."

I paused, trying to think of a response. This was so not what I had expected.

"So… what now?" I asked hesitantly.

Walter glanced down at this watch. "Well, I was thinking maybe, if you don't have any plans tonight, that I could take you out to dinner."

I pretended to ponder the suggestion. "Like a *date*?"

He moved his eyebrows up and down suggestively. "Like a *date*."

"Are you sure you're ready to date?"

"After this past weekend… positive." He came closer, pulling me into him. "And you?"

I glanced over at my cell phone. "After that phone conversation… absolutely."

"Well I just want to be certain," he whispered. "Because I happen to really like the shirt I'm wearing."

I shoved him, laughing. Then I looked up as he leaned in and took my lips in his.

The kiss started out at a slow pace, gradually speeding up, the emotion building as our lips interlocked. It was a different kind of kiss, sexy yet innocent, passionate yet comfortable. The kind of kiss you experience when you start as friends.

His lips were thick and soft and tasted like peppermint. He grasped at my waist, pressing himself against me, his tongue tracing mine. I could feel his heart pounding against my chest. I ran my hands up and down his back, kissing him hard, then soft, then hard again.

When we managed to break free of each other, Walter glanced devilishly towards my bedroom. "You know, it's really too bad you don't have a bed in here yet."

"That's probably a good thing."

"Yeah, I guess you're right." He smoothed his hand over my hair, then glanced at the front door. "Ready to go, beautiful?"

"Let's do it."

He reached out and took my right hand in his left, as we made our way down the hallway and out into the cold Boston night.

Epilogue

Six months later, in late August, Walter and I sat in the backyard of Renee and Dylan's new home, where Beth and Eddie had opted to have their wedding reception. It was a small wedding, about 50 guests, mainly just close friends and family. Dylan and his band mates performed on the back patio, while Renee's cousin Vicki tended bar in the corner. The backyard was just as I'd imagined on the day we'd gone house-hunting – white party lights strung overhead, tiki torch lamps, fire pits, bohemian-style couches, live music echoing through the air.

It was hard to believe Sierra was already six months old. She floated from person to person in her tiny pink dress, as everyone took turns holding her. Her thin, blonde hair was slowly beginning to spiral around her ears, the same shade as Renee's. But her giant, blue eyes were all Dylan's. She'd somehow got a perfect piece of each of them.

Fortunately, Dylan's grudge against Walter had subsided once we'd started dating, so I was allowed to bring him as my date. The two of us made our rounds from the food table (buffet- style, per Beth's request), to the bar, then to the dance floor. Until the dessert came, at which point I lured Walter back to the food table.

"Did I mention how much I love dessert?" I asked him, piling an assortment of tiny cakes and pastries onto my plate. When he didn't answer, I looked over at him, at which point he proceeded to shove a giant slice of white-frosted cake into my face.

"Walter!" I screamed, wiping my cheeks furiously with a napkin. Everyone nearby burst into hysterics.

Walter grinned, shrugging nonchalantly. "Hey, you said you love dessert."

"Aww!" Kat came bouncing over, resting her left hand on my shoulder and her right on Walter's. She looked back and forth between the two of us, smiling like we were a romantic comedy. "You guys are adorable."

"Yeah, I might have had something to do with that," Renee whispered, sneaking up behind us, looking gorgeous in her tight, crimson dress. It was hard to believe she'd just had a baby not too long ago.

I whipped around to face her. "Had something to do with what?" I looked at Walter accusingly. "Tell me that isn't true."

He stood silent, shifting his weight from one foot to the other.

"Oh, come on, you're not glad?" Renee looked at me doubtfully.

Before I could say anything, Walter turned to face Kat. "For the record, I would've asked her out anyway."

I shook my head in disbelief. "When did you…"

"Oh relax," Renee said. "When I called him to tell him we were buying the house, I just casually mentioned that… since you were both single… maybe he should take you out sometime."

I glared at her. She batted her lashes innocently, then looked down at her champagne flute.

"Did I mention how happy I am that I can drink again?" She took a sip from her glass, then turned and skipped away.

"Alright everyone," Dylan announced into the microphone. "This is one of the greatest songs ever written, so if you guys want to grab your date…" He gestured to the center of the yard, where they'd set up a makeshift dance floor.

I recognized the song instantly. It was Jeff Buckley's "Lover You Should've Come Over." The song that had brought Renee and Dylan together. And essentially, had brought Renee and me together, many years ago. Back in our high-school days.

Walter peered at me curiously, taking my hand in his. "Care to dance, my lady?"

My lips twitched as I reluctantly followed him onto the dance floor. It was impossible to be mad at him. All he had to do was flash one of those cute little smiles and I'd completely forget why I was upset in the first place.

I threw my arms around his neck as he pulled me against him, his musky scent lingering. My favorite smell. My safe haven.

It was funny how, in just six months' time, someone could become your everything.

"I can't believe you didn't tell me," I whispered.

"Like I said, I would've asked you out anyway." He peered down at my mint-green satin dress, his eyes grazing me seductively. "Come on, look at you. How could I not?"

"Yeah, yeah."

I leaned into him again, thinking about how much had transpired since I'd met him, how much different my life would be if I'd made another decision. I looked around at my friends, drinking, laughing, swaying back and forth to the music. I'd always love California, but here, I was home. I was where I belonged.

Acknowledgements

First, I'd like to thank everyone from my hometown of Rockland, Massachusetts, for the overwhelming amount of support I've received. Words can't even express how much your encouragement means to me, and I thank all of you from the bottom of my heart.

I'd also like to thank all the new friends I've made in Los Angeles in the past five years, some of which helped inspire the new characters in this book. It's incredible how much your life can change in such a short time, and I'm fortunate to have such great people in my life.

As always, I'm extremely grateful to all my friends and family members who have been there since the beginning. My dream never would've came true without all of you by my side.

And last, a giant thank you to the wonderful team at Harper Impulse, for being so amazingly easy to work with. I couldn't ask for a better team.